a king wong adventure

THE GURU GIRL GAMBIT

jim jackson

元朗
綿綿冰
糖水甜品專門店
NEW
DELHI

Nik
九龍生活攝影器材
盈興隆
RANT (麵家)
餐廳
End
終止
翡翠茶餐
JADE RESTAURA
盈興隆
海味
九

PRAIRIE SOUL PRESS

Cover credit:
CSA Images/Color Printstock Collection istock.com
ID: 152406010

Photo credits:
Annie Spratt on unsplash.com
Richard Lee on unsplash.com

ISBN-13: 978-1-7771293-2-3

With a nod to Marie Kondo – if I hadn't decluttered my life, I never would have started writing again. I hope she doesn't mind the mild jab!

多利來

1

Hong Kong is a place where the stuff of the world washes up. From the cheap plastic toys of Mainland factories to expat's beloved mementos of home cast off when a better job elsewhere calls, Hong Kong swallows it all into its tiny geography.

And sometimes it gets chucked back up.

I'd spent the better part of the night chasing a sentient, one-legged umbrella.

That's right.

Umbrella.

I was the world's only exoterric consultant and expert on the Otherkind who boil up from the Borderlands and live in the cracks and holes our human, Foursquare world refuses to see. I was the one who could see them all. And I was the one who could hold back the nastier ones that threatened polite society.

And on this fine night in early May, that meant chasing a hopping, living umbrella past a security guard gasping in fear and through the hanging bags of the deserted Goldfish Market in Mongkok.

"Hey, *pang yau,*" I called out among the oblivious goldfish in their plastic bags. "I know you're a long way from home. Why don't we just talk about a plan to get you back where you belong?"

"No belong," a fluttering, inhuman voice called from somewhere behind a row of fish. "Cast away."

I pushed my hat back on my head. "That's the modern world, pal. We've all been cast away by someone sometime." I darted around a corner, sure I'd see the thing. No dice. "I should tell you about this Malaysian woman I met on the KCR just past Kowloon Tong station. She cast me off like a –"

A wire frame of goldfish bags pummelled the ground, bags bursting and casting flopping fish onto the concrete. Beyond the flapping fish bodies, a flutter of motion – a hopping umbrella bouncing deeper into the maze of the market.

I lurched to follow, but my eyes caught the pleading looks of goldfish.

"*Yiu!*" I spat and collected what I could into my arms. I tossed them into a drip bucket under an air-conditioning unit and looked at my sodden linen suit.

"I should have asked for more cash for this hopped-up case."

I followed the trail of burst fish bags, saving who I could, into the back of the market.

No exit signs here. Just smooth concrete walls and darkness.

And quiet. A whole lorry-load of quiet that I didn't expect from my flailing umbrella friend.

"*Pang yau?*" I called into the dim. "How about we find you a home, eh? Someplace nice. With a cozy stand. And … whatever else umbrellas like."

I heard a quick flap. "You no know me. I hunger. You no know what I like."

I pushed my hat back on my head. "On the contrary, *pang yau*. I know you, and I can name you." I pulled my hat down. "And I've got a feeling that naming you will pull the living right out of that old umbrella."

Another flap. "You kill me?"

"Well. No. Maybe. I guess. But come on. You're an umbrella."

"I living being," its voice echoed off the concrete.

"Living, sure. But *being*? I think I covered that when I said you're an umbrella."

"No kill."

I pulled a well-chewed pencil from my pocket and took a

long drag. It was a poor substitute for the pack of cigarettes I used to smoke every day. "I don't want to." Another drag. "Don't make me."

A sudden flapping, and the thing flapped in front of me and opened, pinning me against more bags of oblivious goldfish.

"No kill," it hissed at me. Its one eye, bleary and bloodshot, stared me down.

I let the pencil fall from my lips. "Like I said – don't make me."

Its eye narrowed. "Friend?"

"Friend." I pushed my hat back on my head. "Conditionally. I can't have you hopping around, terrorizing Foursquares, can I, *pang yau?* You nearly dealt a coronary to that night watchman back there. Didn't your mother ever tell you it's rude to jump out screaming at people like that? Especially when you're a one-eyed umbrella with a two-foot-long tongue."

Its tongue flicked out and licked the corners of my mouth. "I no like humans."

"No one does, I've found. But they outnumber you Otherkind a hundred to one. Probably best to get along with them." I pushed the flicking tongue away. "They'll do bad things to you if you don't."

"No!" the umbrella shrieked and flapped. "I live." It hopped directly over me, through the rows of fish and out the door.

"*Yiu!* You couldn't just make this easy, could you?" I pulled my hat down and followed.

The thing was fully open, pinning a shirtless, down-on-his-luck guy against a wall. The wiry little joker reached out for his trove of treasures, but couldn't reach the shopping trolley he carted them around in.

"Don't make me do this, *pang yau*."

It licked the guy with its long tongue, and he stiffened.

"I live."

"Not at the cost of these people."

It cast its eye to the beggar. "He nothing. Cast away. Unwanted. Like me. No one care if he die."

I pulled my hat down. "I care."

Its tongue licked at the corners of the guy's mouth. "I hunger."

"We all do, chuckles. Some of us are content with cheap Seven-Eleven dim sum. Others want to gobble down harmless passersby, and I need to stop them. Where do you fall along that line?"

It opened its gaping mouth. The guy cringed.

I pushed my hat back. "Seriously? It's going down this way? Fine." I reached into my back pocket, pulled out my Moleskine notebook and found the well-thumbed page I needed. "I call on you, Otherkind of the Borderlands, by your true name – *Kasa-obake*."

The thing snapped its mouth shut and turned its bleary eye to me.

Then fell lifeless to the ground.

I pulled my hat down.

The guy kow-towed a couple times to me, then turned to flee. He stopped, looked down at the old umbrella and tossed it into his cart.

I stepped out onto Bute Street and down into the throbbing artery of Nathan Road just beginning to pulse with early morning business, already mentally spending the handful of cash I'd get for returning a little old lady's little old umbrella.

2

I walked past the accumulated junk of the day set out for morning trash pickup. Things and stuff piled up in front of shuttered business, both legitimate and otherwise, half obscured the sidewalk.

After a groaning lift in the Kwok Wing building, I found my client's door and knocked. I heard the shuffling and thumping of elderly feet walking grumpily to answer an unwanted door.

"Yes?" the old woman said, squinting.

I pushed my hat back. "It's all taken care of Mrs. Lee. Your old umbrella won't be bothering anyone anymore."

She leaned in closer and squinted harder. "Where is?"

"Where is what? The umbrella? Don't worry. It's in safe hands."

"I want."

"You want the umbrella?" I pulled my hat down. "After it trashed your place and licked you silly?"

"I want. Is mine."

"Look, doll – you hired me to take care of a living umbrella. I did. The bill is two thousand, four hundred and fifty. How would you like to pay?"

"No pay." She turned to close the door. I jammed a foot in it.

"Yes pay. Now if you wouldn't mind."

"No pay. No umbrella, no pay."

"How could you possibly want that thing back?"

"Is mine."

"*Yiu!* People and their stuff. You cast it off, then want it back. Even if comes to life and licks you."

"No umbrella, no pay."

She shoved the door repeatedly, pinching my aching foot in sharp metal.

"Is mine. No umbrella, no pay."

She shoved the door again, and I put a stern hand on it.

"Two thousand, four hundred and fifty." I pulled my hat down farther. "Cash is best."

I heard the lift groan before I registered that I was shaking down an old lady for cash in her own apartment.

"*Jau man tai ma?*" a comically large gym rat said. "We got a problem here?"

I turned and pushed by hat back. "Nothing I can't handle. Thanks, though, chuckles."

His hallway-wide shoulders scraped past me. "Mrs. Lee? This *kai zi* bothering you?"

"No pay. No umbrella, no pay."

The *Kuafu* giant turned to me and puffed out his chest in my face. "You heard the lady, friend. If you don't give her back her umbrella, you don't get paid."

"She doesn't want the umbrella."

"Is mine."

"Sounds like she does."

I stepped toward the giant, and my foot slipped from the door. It closed hard.

I pulled my hat down. "*Yiu!* That was my horse race money."

Giant man looked me over. "How much could you possibly get for returning a lost umbrella?"

"Two thousand, four hundred and fifty."

"What? She wouldn't just buy a new umbrella?"

"It's not like that, chuckles."

He puffed out his chest farther. "What's it like then, friend?"

"Her umbrella was a legendary Japanese *Kasa-obake* – a living umbrella that chucked out umbrellas turn into. One eye, one foot. And a nasty tongue. It's hopped up."

"You're nuts."

"I've been called worse, pal."

"You get superstitious old ladies to believe this stuff about living umbrellas with tongues, then charge them thousands of dollars to deal with the problem? That's extortion in my books." He rolled up his sleeves, showing an intricate tattoo of a tiger fighting a dragon that extended up the length of his arm. Triad marks, if I'd ever seen them.

I pushed my hat back and shot him what I hoped was a charming smile. "I'm not looking for any trouble, chuckles. How about I just cut my losses and be on my way?"

"So you can bilk other grannies of their tea money?" He shot a more charming smile that told me in no uncertain terms the depths of violence he was about to unleash. "I don't think so, friend."

I pulled my hat down. "Would it change your mind if I told you that I won the Wushu Kung Fu championship these last three years running? You don't know what you're getting into."

His smile deepened to a grin. "You didn't win the Wushu Kung Fu championship the last three years running."

"How would you know, chuckles?"

"Because *I* won the Wushu Kung Fu championship the last three years running."

"Oh. Gotcha."

He stepped forward. "Are we going to do this or what?"

"I vote no."

"Good thing this isn't a democracy." He shot a look around the apartment doors. "But I don't feel like disturbing my neighbours. Shall we go downstairs?"

"I'm good here."

"It wasn't a question, friend."

"No, I suppose not."

He gestured to the lift. "After you?"

I took a few shuffling steps, then darted to the lift button. It opened, and I slipped in.

I shot ape man a smile and pushed my hat back. "Actually chuckles, why don't you take the next one?"

He stepped forward, and I hammered the ground floor button.

The door groaned and thought about closing.

I hammered some more.

He kept walking.

Old metal groaned across my eyeline, obscuring my view of the beast. I breathed again.

Until a meaty paw shot through the crack and shoved the door open.

I only saw his grin. I didn't see the ham fist shoot out and connect hard with my nose. I didn't see the spurt of blood that decorated the lift. I didn't see stars or chirping birdies as I slipped into sweet, dark unconsciousness.

3

They say there's a fine line between success and failure. If that's true, I'd always been well south of that line. I don't know how many times I'd ridden up and down in that lift before I came to. By the time I'd made it through the clutter of Nathan Road, I felt like I'd been hit by a double-decker night bus. And robbed. A hard ache settled somewhere between the back of my eyes and my thoracic vertebrae.

I threw open the door to the back room of the Violet Eyes bar – my poor excuse for something to call *home* – pulled my hat over my eyes and flopped onto the folding cot that passed for a place to lay my head.

I heard voices over the hum of the refrigerator. Dames.

"Put it to your lips," an unfamiliar voice said.

"Like this?" a more familiar voice said.

"No *press* your lips against it. Ah there. Oh yes. Do you feel its bliss?"

The familiar voice muffled out a response.

Sterner now. "I said do you feel its bliss? When you press it to your lips, do you feel it?"

"Maybe?"

I pushed my hat back on my head, gave up on trying to wrestle any sleep from the day and went to see what was going on. I had no idea what to expect. But I had some preferences.

"Jaz?" I called out as I opened the door to the main room. "Am I disturbing anything?"

She waved from a far corner of the bar. "King. Come here and meet someone. She's *awesome.*"

I was skeptical. "I'm skeptical."

"No, seriously. This is life-changing."

I pulled my hat down. "I like my life unchanged, thanks."

Jaz cast her eyes up and down my fraying linen suit, the deep purple under my eyes and abstract art splooge of blood on my rumpled shirt. "Oh yeah?"

"Yeah."

"Come meet her anyway."

A Korean woman stood up beside Jaz – tall, smooth and elegant for her youth.

"Pleased to meet you, Mr. Wong. I'm Bong-Cha Gim. I've heard so much about what you do. Oh yes."

I shot Jaz a look. "Jasmine? Have you been telling the lady

about my business?"

Bong-Cha didn't give her a chance to respond.

"Ah there. No tricks of the trade or anything like that. Oh yes, your secrets are safe. But we are in similar lines of work, Mr. Wong."

"Oh, are we?"

"Ah there. I can see by the sourness on your face that you're skeptical. Of course, I'm no esoteric consultant. That honour is purely yours."

"Exoterric. With two *R*s."

"Excuse me?"

"I'm an exoterric consultant."

She cocked her head. "Exoteric? As in, plain. Ordinary."

"I spell it with two *R*s. It means *out of this world*."

"Ah there. But don't you always need to explain how you spell it? Wouldn't it make more sense to call yourself an *esoteric* consultant?"

I'd formed a strong opinion of this dame. "Nope."

"No?"

"You call yourself what you want, doll." I pulled my hat down. "And I'll call yourself what *I* want."

"Ah there."

Jaz cut through the tension with some hippie-psychology. "King – you should really listen to the Bong-Cha Gim system. It's totally cleansing."

I pushed my hat back at looked to Bong-Cha. "You've got a system."

"Ah there. I've got a system. To make lives simple and free."

"For canning tomatoes? You'll make a fortune."

Jaz stood up and slapped my arm. "That's not nice."

Bong-Cha took it in stride. My opinion of her waffled. "I have a system for changing your life through the simple act of decluttering."

"Decluttering? Like chucking out stuff you don't use?" I smiled. "You won't get rich doing that, doll."

She ran a long-fingered hand down her thigh to smooth her black dress. Last year, I broke the one-million-dollar mark."

"You did, huh?" My impression of her got real solid real fast. "A million Hong Kong dollars is nothing to sneeze at."

"A million US dollars, Mr. Wong. Oh yes."

I pulled my hat down. "You made a million US teaching people to chuck out their old junk?" I looked her up and down. "There isn't a little more to it? Come on. What's really going on?"

"Ah there. You're not the first one to be skeptical of my system. People are suffocating under the weight of their accumulated possessions. Drowning, unable to stop buying. Possessions breed more possessions, just as toxin craves more toxin. Oh yes. My system frees them from the cycle of stuff and allows them to find their material Nirvana."

I pushed my hat back and caught Jaz's look begging me not to openly insult our guest. "Alright, I'll bite." I sat down. "How do you get people to give up their tat and trinkets?"

She ran a hand down her thigh again. I didn't see a wrinkle to smooth. "My system is very simple. It's about bliss."

I leaned back in my chair. "Back to my point about this whole thing being a front."

She leaned forward, closing again the space between us. "Ah there. You're talking about sexual bliss. Oh yes. There is that." Her voice got low and husky. "But if that's the only bliss you've tasted, you're missing out."

"And you can show me, I take it?"

"I can show you."

"For a fee."

"Ah there. For others there would be a fee. For you, *gratis*."

Jaz bounced in her seat. "That's what I've been trying to tell you, King. Bong-Cha is going to declutter our lives in exchange for an honest review. Isn't that awesome?" Her voice lowered. "Maybe get rid of that old box of Mei Hu's stuff."

"No. She's coming back."

Jaz knitted her brow. "No one else seems to think so."

I pulled my hat down. "What's the system?"

Bong-Cha leaned in closer to me. "Take off your hat."

I smiled. "Wow. You get real intimate real fast, don't you?"

I took off my hat and handed it to her.

She recoiled.

"Ah there. I'd rather not touch something like that. It's you who must apply the system. Put your hat to your lips."

I did. I smelled sweat and hair oil.

"No," Bong-Cha said. "No *press* your lips against it." She reached out and shoved my hat to my mouth, rubbing the straw in circles against me. "Ah there. Oh yes. Do you feel its bliss?"

I didn't want to admit it, but there certainly was a warmth I got from this old thing. The good times. The rainy times. All the times my hat had been there for me.

Bliss.

I stood up and put it back on my head. "Sorry, doll. I didn't feel a thing." I shot a glance at my watch. "But you go ahead and declutter all the bliss out of my assistant here. I've got a meeting with a potential client."

I could hear Jaz's explanations and remonstrations start, but I was up the stairs and out into the heat and press of Nathan Road.

4

Rodney Lau was your typical absent-minded professor. Well, no. He kept the cluttered desk, stained teacups, wild hair, and threadbare corduroy, but he mixed that with a good three fingers of pants-on-his-head, thinking-he's-a-lamppost looniness. He taught a class about the psychology of consumerism at the business school attached to Hong Kong University of Science and Technology. Go figure.

"Demons, King," he said too loudly and pulled at his wild white hair. "Demons, I say."

I skirted a stack of three-year-old newspapers and pulled my Moleskine notebook from my back pocket. "Demons, you say?"

"I say demons."

I took a long, unsatisfying drag from my pencil. "Chasing you?"

"Chasing me, I say."

"Huh." I pulled my hat down. "Have you seen them?"

He pulled at his hair and stared at me. "Seen?"

"The demons. Have you seen them?"

"Seen the demons? Well. No." He widened his stare and got in real close. "But they're chasing me, King. Demons, I say."

"But you haven't seen them?"

"Seen. No. I haven't seen them."

"So they could, honestly, be rats. Or – and I'm just spitballing here – they could be nothing. Just in your head. Isn't that right?"

He pressed the bridge of his nose against mine, his eyes opened wild. "Possible," he whispered. "But not true. There are demons chasing me. Demons, I say. You still believe your lost wife is coming back – is that all in your head?"

I pulled my face away. "Okay. Let's play. Why?"

"Why?" His eyes slit. "Why what?"

"Why are these demons chasing you?" I leaned forward with an eager look, ready to write in my notebook.

"Why? I hadn't thought of *why*. It's not my job to think of *why*. That's why I hire you."

"Fair point." I took another drag of my pencil. "Any thoughts that could point me in a direction, though? Anything you have that demons might want a piece of?"

"From me?"

“Since they’re chasing you.” I pushed my hat back. “Any ideas what they want?”

“It’s my knowledge, I say.” He tapped the side of his head, and his finger got caught in the wires of white hair.

“Your knowledge.” I put my notebook away. “Of consumer psychology.”

He kept tapping with the trapped finger. “Of consumer psychology.”

“What – are the demons looking to do some market research?”

“Perhaps. Mine is not to reason why.”

“I hate to break it to you Dr. Rodney – we go back a long way – but that’s not been my experience with demons.” I pulled my hat down and shoved my well-chewed pencil in my pocket. “I don’t think I can help you much. It’s –”

A shot of blue flame erupted from a stained teacup on the cluttered desk. I grabbed Dr. Rodney and pulled him to the floor.

The flames were gone.

I pushed my hat back on my head. “Does that happen to you a lot?”

“Twice a week, King. Twice a week, I say.”

“Huh.” I stood up and dusted myself off. “Maybe there’s something to this, after all.” I shot him a look. “At the regular price, right?”

"Of course, of course."

I heard a shuffling in the broom closet in the corner of the office. "Gotcha you little *kai zi*."

I yanked opened the door.

Nothing.

But an old umbrella.

I shuddered and closed the door.

A clunk in the hall, and I slipped through the door into the bare white hall. "Wait here," I said to Dr. Rodney.

"Of course, King. I don't want to follow a demon. I don't want to, I say."

The sleek lines of steel and glass that made up this floor of the school were marred by a single chair in the middle of the hall.

And old, wooden chair with a broken leg.

"That shouldn't be," I said to no one and pulled down my hat.

I walked up slowly, carefully. Then I shot a glance around to see if anyone saw me wary of an old wooden chair with a missing leg.

"I'm scared of splinters," I said to anyone who might have been hiding in the bare hall. "Nasty things."

I kicked a good leg of the chair.

It didn't bite.

I kicked another one.

It stood up.

The chair straightened up nine feet and transformed into a man-monster with black tattoos crisscrossing its blue skin and single leg. Its back carried the shell of a turtle, and it snapped at me with a sharp beak that shot out from its craggy dome head.

Okay, I didn't see that coming.

I swallowed the pounding in my heart and stuck out a hand. "King Wong, exoterric consultant – pleased to meet you." I pushed my hat back. "You're not from around here, are you? I'd recognize a handsome devil like you. What brings you to Hong Kong, *pang yau?*"

It locked me in cold blue eyes.

"You." Its voice sounded like splintering wood. "You are the one we were warned about. The fool king. The bumbling hero."

I took my hand back unshaken. "I don't know about where you're from, chuckles, but on my street those names border on offensive."

"No matter," it continued. "I will end you here before you can threaten my brethren as foretold."

"Pal, if I had Star Ferry fare for every two-bit hobgoblin and toothed dust bunny who threatened to end me, I'd be over here in Central way more often." I pulled my hat down. "Well. No. I wouldn't. I don't like it here. What I'm trying to say is that jokers like you threaten to end me a lot. Enough that I'd remark on it." I looked up into its cold eyes. "That doesn't sound as tough. Can I start again?"

In response, the beast only snapped open its beak and shot a long, snaking tongue through razor teeth.

"Maybe I'll just go," I said and turned to run.

5

Memory is a tricky thing. We look back at scenes in our lives as if we have an objective recording of them. But memories are made up of feelings and assumptions and worries and hopes. Not facts. And, just as emotions fade and change at the touch of a lover or slap of an ex-lover, memories can shift and change at the hands of Otherkind who know how to manipulate them.

I turned from a blue, nine-foot-tall man-monster with beak and turtle shell, but I didn't see it. No. That's not right. I didn't *remember* it. And, since memory is all we have once the thing itself leaves our view, when I turned to run, I had no idea why I was running.

I blinked and looked around the steel and glass of the hall, wondering why my heart was pounding and why the words *not yet – the time is not right* echoed in my adrenaline-shot head.

I looked back to the broken chair.

“Am I that scared of splinters?” I said to no one and headed back to Dr. Rodney’s office.

“Look, Doc,” I said and pushed my hat back, lifting my legs to find places to put my feet in the collected clutter, still tripping over a pile of ashtrays full of vintage ash. “I didn’t find anything.”

I thought of turtles and birds and blue, and again I heard the words *not yet – the time is not right* in my head.

“You didn’t find the demons?”

“I don’t think there are any demons, Doc.” I looked around at the collected junk cluttering his space. “I think this might be like the time you called because there was a nine-tailed fox living in your bathroom.”

“That was a hard time for me.”

“I know, Doc. But you remember what it was, right?”

“Of course I do. I say, you just said it – a nine-tailed fox.”

I pulled out my pencil and took a long drag. “That’s what you *thought* it was. I investigated. Do you remember what I found?”

“A nine-tailed –”

“No. What it *really* was.”

His eyes searched the ceiling for the memory. He found it, and his eyes got wide. “Oh, I say.”

“What was it, Doc? What did you think was a nine-tailed fox?”

"Of course – that old towel in the corner."

I took another unsatisfying drag from my pencil. "That old towel in the corner. But you were so sure."

"I'm sure about being chased by demons, too."

"I know you are. Just like the towel."

He pulled at his hair. "Is it just like the towel, King?"

"I think so, Doc. I think so." I looked again at the stacks of books and take-out containers. The newspapers and candy wrappers. The pens and tape rolls and homemade DVDs. The artificial plants stacked on themselves, vying for light they don't even need. And the endless papers that dusted everything in the room like snow.

I heard words in my head again but in a different voice – that hopped-up decluttering dame. *People are suffocating under the weight of their accumulated possessions. Drowning, unable to stop buying. Possessions breed more possessions, just as toxin craves more toxin.*

I took my hat off, looked for a surface to put it down on then put it back on. "I think the state of this office might be affecting you, *pang yau*." I grabbed a shopping bag from a pile in the corner. "What do you say we clean up a little? I think it might help with your demon problem."

"I say, you think it will help?"

"I really do." I tossed out a load of take-out containers.

We cleaned – what I wouldn't have given for a pair of

rubber gloves – and we talked.

“Tell me about consumer psychology, Doc? Why do people buy the things they buy?”

“Fascinating question, King. I say, fascinating. It’s not from desire, as one would think. Oh, no. We want what we want not because we want it.”

“Eh?”

“It’s about group identification. We want what we want because what we want makes us feel we belong to the group of our choosing.”

I pulled my hat down and chucked a bagful of mostly broken knick-knacks into the hall.

A column of blue flame shot up from the middle of the hall where I’d tossed the bag, and a lanky blue man-monster snapped a toothy beak at me.

“*Yiu!*” I spat and shot a look at Dr. Rodney.

When I turned back, the thing was gone. So was my memory of having seen it.

“I don’t follow, Doc.” I pushed my hat back and thought of beaks and teeth for some reason. “We buy things to feel part of a group?”

“I say, yes, King. We can pay thirty dollars for a cup of gourmet coffee because we want to be part of the group that pays thirty dollars for a cup of gourmet coffee. Or, we buy two-dollar tea at a hole-in-the-wall because we want to be part of the group that does that." He pulled at the wires of his hair. "No one wants to be excluded, so we find our groups. No one wants to be cast off."

"Gotcha." I tossed a trash bag of collected junk into the hall. "I guess I don't care to be part of a group."

Dr. Rodney grabbed me by the shoulders and stared into my eyes. "Don't say that, King. I say, not even you want to be cast off. Find your group. Be part of it. Follow the group's flow even if it's not your own desire. That is how we stave off the madness of being alone and cast off."

I thought of Jaz and her hopped-up decluttering plan. "Fine, Doc." I pulled my hat down. "I'll see what I can do."

I pulled away from him and looked around the office. It wasn't spotless, but I could see the desk.

"Not a bad job, huh Doc? I bet you're feeling better already."

He smiled. I hadn't seen him do that in years. "Better, King. I say, still a little worried about those demons chasing me."

"I get it. Tell you what – I know someone. Someone who can help finish what we started here. I'll bring her by."

I let myself out the door.

"Find your group, King," he called after me. "Don't be cast off."

As I walked down the clean, sleek hall of steel and glass, I didn't hear the screams of a man who was good to me when no one else could find a reason to be.

6

Crossing between Kowloon and Central on the Star Ferry isn't my idea of fun at the best of times. Doing it with an ice-cold decluttering dame is near-torture. With each slosh of the boat on the wakes of the giant container ships, my gut tightened.

"Oh yes, Mr. Wong – the method is really quite easy. You press each of your belongings to your lips – kiss them, as it were. If you don't feel its bliss with the kiss, cast it off. Thus leaving your life simple and free."

I pulled my hat down and looked and the chop of the harbour tossing around cast-off plastic baubles and trashed wrappers of trinkets prized for a minute then junked, too. "I've got belongings that wouldn't be sanitary if I kissed them."

"It's very easy to be cynical, isn't it, Mr. Wong?"

"Works for me, doll."

"Does it? Because I look at you and see a man suffocating

under the weight of his own clutter."

I turned to her. "I live on a cot in the back room of a downstairs bar in Chungking Mansions. I don't have room for a lot of clutter."

"Ah there. You still assume I mean physical objects."

My eyebrow shot up. "What else are you offering to declutter?"

"Your soul."

I felt a shot of something warm in my chest. Probably heartburn from my last Chungking Mansions samosa. "I sold that years ago, doll."

"No."

I pushed my hat back. "No? *No* what?"

"No, you didn't sell your soul." She ran a hand down her thigh. "I can see it. I can see it through the clutter of pain and experience and broken hopes and lost loves." She reached out and ran a hand down my thigh. "Can't you see through your own clutter?"

I looked back to the water. "Maybe I need glasses."

"Cut through the clutter. It will change your life. Oh yes."

"Like I said – I like my life the way it is."

She looked again at my fraying shirt and the purple bags I lugged around under my eyes. "I can make you better."

"A better me and two-twenty will get you a ride on the lower deck of the Star Ferry."

"Ah there. Peeling back the clutter around your heart and your soul will show you who you truly are."

I pulled my hat down. "Maybe I don't want to be shown who I really am."

She squeezed my thigh. "You do. You will."

I turned to her. The ice queen exterior had melted, and I swore I saw a scamper of real affection in her eyes. A vibration somewhere in the bottom of my chest hummed in unison with whatever hopped-up vibe she was putting out.

"We're here," I said as the ferry sloshed into Central terminal. "It's not far to the university."

She pulled her hand from my leg and stood up.

"Hey, doll?"

She turned.

I pushed my hat back on my head. "Thanks for helping me with Dr. Rodney. He was good to me when no one else could find a reason to be. And he's not … he's not doing too great."

The affection scampered across her eyes again. "It's my pleasure, Mr. Wong. My life's work is to free people of the clutter that traps them." She leaned and whispered in my ear. "And this way I can see you in your natural habitat. I need to know what you look like bare and stripped of the clutter that covers you."

"Bare and stripped, eh? I think I may have some old Polaroids …"

But she was gone, hipswaying up the gangway. I followed.

And then.

The hoards.

If I didn't know better, I'd have thought the dame had just been squeezed in a multi-armed hug from the goddess Doumu and carried lovingly to Nirvana.

But no. These were Foursquares – a couple hundred of them thronging the ramp up from the ferry's gangway, each shrieking in Beatlemania dog-whistle tones, waving pens and autograph books.

And Bong-Cha dutifully – without burden or eye rolls – signed her name for each insipid, adoring fan. She stooped to conquer the hearts of these peons so far beneath her grace.

Huh. Maybe that's the calmness that comes with living an uncluttered existence. Simple and free.

I pulled my hat down. If so, she can keep it.

I elbowed, shouldered and kneed through the throng of aspirationals. "Okay, okay, that's enough," I called over dog-whistle shrieks. "*Gau lak.* Give the lady some room." I pushed my hat back. "Hey, why don't we try a little something. Those autograph books – press them to your lips."

They shot me puzzled looks as if their very existence had just been jigsawed.

"Just do it. Press them to your lips. Um … *kiss* them."

"Ah there," Bong-Cha said behind me. "Oh yes."

A couple hundred notebooks pressed against a couple hundred mouths. I gagged silently.

"Do you feel its bliss?" The words caught in my throat. "Well, do you?"

I watched puzzled faces twist and harden into disgust.

"That's what I thought." I pushed my hat back. "So? What are you waiting for? Cast them away. That's what you've gotta do if you can't feel its bliss, *deoi bat deoi?*"

Slowly, it crept over them like ivy cluttering the side of perfectly good brick wall. And they obeyed.

A couple hundred autograph books fluttered off the side of Central Pier and slopped into Victoria Harbour's fetid water to join the other discarded junk.

"There – now doesn't that feel better?" I pulled my hat down and turned to Bong-Cha. "Say goodbye to your little friends. We've got places to be."

"Ah there. That was a wicked thing to do, Mr. Wong," she said in a totally un-disapproving way. "To take advantage of those poor people's desire to live a life simple and free."

"I've been called way worse things than *wicked*, doll." I pushed my hat back and shot her a smile. "But I sure could get used to swinging around that kind of power. You must like it – being able to shape your world the way you want it."

Her head drooped. "I only try to help. Oh yes."

"You don't get off on the power? Not even a little?"

“I only –” a catch in her voice “ – I only try to help.”

“Huh.” I pulled my hat down, and we strode into the cacophony of concrete and sweaty flesh that was Central’s financial district.

7

We walked the fifteen minutes through the jungle of people, trams and chaotic motion of Central. Bong-Cha stopped and turned to me.

"Your friend – how badly is he suffering?"

I pulled my hat down. "Pretty bad, doll."

She smiled to the distance.

"That's funny?" I said.

"Ah there. No, it's awful. What I find funny is that you even clutter your speech. Why not speak simple and free? These words – *doll*, *pal* – serve no purpose but to clutter your meaning and hide yourself from others."

"That's a pretty good purpose, if you ask me."

She pressed a hand to my shoulder. "Show yourself, Mr. Wong. At least to me."

"You don't want to so see what I've got under these stylish

duds."

A street vendor hawking newly minted ancient coins hawked loudly in our direction. Bong-Cha startled halfway into my arms. Her ice-queen schtick melted some under the May heat or my irresistible charm.

I pushed my hat back. "*Yiu!* It looks like the Mainland factories are stepping up production of cheap, meaningless stuff. You're not in cahoots with the Chinese government, are you? They produce it, people buy it, get overwhelmed by clutter, and call on you?"

She pulled from me, ignoring the question. "All the more reason to find things that, when pressed to your lips, you can feel their bliss."

"You're always going on about finding bliss *in* the thing. Shouldn't we look for things that bring *us* bliss?"

The ice queen in her frosted over hard again. "Ah there. Spoken like a man."

"It sure was. Straight from my big, masculine baritone."

She turned and glared frosty death rays at me. "All you care about is what you can *get* from things. You don't care what you do to them. Or how they *feel*."

I slipped off my hat and scratched what was left of my hair. "Yep, you hit the nail pretty much right on the head, doll. When it comes to inanimate objects, I really only care about how I can use them."

"Oh yes. It clutters your very language. You speak of hitting nails – an act of pure violence."

I scratched harder at my scalp. "Uh … isn't that what nails are for?"

"Ah there. A typical man."

I slapped my hat on my head and pulled it down. "Maybe you need a bit of typical man in your … life."

She swung in front of me and planted herself hard and straight on the steaming pavement. "You don't know what I need. I need nothing from you or your kind. It's your kind who run the factories that pollute pure and uncluttered lives with mere *things*. It's your kind who create false demand by insisting objects will bring peace and prosperity. And it's your kind who sell the tat and trash to fulfill that demand. It's your kind –"

"It's my kind you're secretly attracted to." I pushed my hat back. "Admit it – you'd love to trip over my collected clutter on the way to my bed." I swallowed hard, trying to think of something more to get her goat. "My bed, which is … also cluttered."

A shriek as dog-whistle high as the wail of her fans erupted from somewhere deep in her uncluttered throat. "Mr. Wong – I'll have you know that I keep my romantic life as uncluttered as the rest of my life." She swallowed hard, trying to think of something more to get my goat. "And, when I bring something to my lips, I can *always* feel its bliss."

I pulled my hat down and shouldered past her up the university's sleek steps. "Dr. Rodney's office is just down here."

She followed close enough behind me I could still feel her frost.

Dr. Rodney's door hung open, and the hairs on the back of my neck shot up.

I shot a look at Bong-Cha. "Wait here."

"What's wrong?"

I pulled my hat down further over my eyes. "Something. Maybe."

I saw first the bareness of the room – no teacups on the desk, no papers on the filing cabinets, no meaningless tat and trash he thought might come in useful someday. The clutter was gone – it was far cleaner than I'd left it. Had the old guy kept on going? Good. That would help him.

Then I saw the body.

Dr. Rodney was splayed out behind the desk, hands still in the wires of his white hair. Even face-down, I could see the terror in his pale body. His tense legs and arched back showed me he died in primal, human fear of something beyond his comprehension. Visions of blue flames, of turtles and of beaks shot across my brain and were gone.

I took off my linen jacket, covered him with it and slipped

back out into the hall.

Bong-Cha smoothed her dress and looked up at me.

"Dead, doll." I ran finger and thumb across my eyes.

"I'm so sorry." She looked away. "Would an embrace ease your pain?"

"What?" I took my hat off and scratched my head.

She swallowed hard. "I'm asking if you need … a hug."

I slapped my hat down on my head and shot my eyes to her. "No. A hug won't do it this time."

"I wouldn't think so."

"And what would you think?" I said through the catch in my throat.

"You want to find out what did this to him."

I looked away. "I should have been here. I shouldn't have left."

"*Should* is a word that only serves to clutter our souls with toxic expectations and false boundaries. You were doing what you thought best. You were helping a friend."

"Fat lot of good it did."

She smoothed her dress and said nothing.

Instead, she put her arms around my shoulders and pressed me to her as I fought back the sobs that threatened to shake me open in the sleek steel and glass of the bare hallway.

二
多利來

8

Two blocks up from teeming Chungking Mansions, there used to be a bookstore. It closed – at least the one upstairs that sold Foursquare books closed – replaced by a discount cosmetics joint. But it wasn't animal-tested eyeliner I was here for after ditching Bong-Cha back in Central.

A tiny shopgirl short-stepped up to me. "Can I … help you, sir?"

"I need Leng Cha Fa."

The worry on the kid's face turned to outright panic.

I pulled my hat down. "Now. *Maa soeng*. I don't have time for pretending she doesn't exist right underneath this place."

The girl gave me a weak smile. She pulled out her phone, snapped a picture of me and started typing. "Well?" I said.

The girl looked up from her phone. "She says you look tired, but you can go down and see her."

"Much obliged, doll. *Doh jie.*"

I slipped to the back corner of the shop where a lift opened, small and cramped.

But inside.

Inside was different.

I smelled it as soon as I got on – the deep forest. Cedar, sage and wet life.

As the lift went down, it expanded onto the forest. Gnarled trees grew from the walls, and leaves on the floor crunched under my feet.

The lift doors opened, but there was no lift left. Just the dense, cool forest, its foliage obscuring the mouth of a deep cave.

A shock of orange fur shot through the undergrowth trailing multiple tails.

The incense fog of the cave was cool and thick. A carved door stood ahead of me. I pushed it open without knocking.

She stood, leaning against a wall of books that went up twenty feet to the top of the cave, dressed in her orange fur corset and sheer, draping skirt, showing the ivory of her legs. Her dark hair framed the white of her face and the blood red of her lips.

Her small, full mouth smiled at me when I walked in, and she brushed hair behind her ear.

"King, lover," she said low and slow. "We were just talking

about you."

I pushed my hat back on my head, suddenly feeling the heat. "Cha Fa, you flatter me."

She smiled that slow smile again and pressed her hands into the small of her back. "Oh, lover. I *can't* flatter you." She leaned forward, and her breasts shook in their fur corset. "You're just *that* good. Mei Hu was one lucky fox spirit."

I took a beat to let it all sink in before I spoke. "Now that we've got the preliminaries out of the way … hey – what do mean *we* were just talking about me?"

She sidled across the room to me as slowly as she smiled. "Your friend came to see me, lover. To ask about you." She leaned in and whispered in my ear. "But I didn't tell her *everything*."

I pulled my hat down. "Friend? *Her?*"

From behind a high shelf, Bong-Cha stepped out and smoothed her dress.

I shot her a look. "What are you doing here?"

Cha Fa leaned on my shoulder and toyed with my earlobe. "I told you, lover. She came to ask about you. But we've mostly been talking about how we can declutter the Underlibrary here."

I shot another look at Bong-Cha. "Seriously? You're trying to tidy the greatest repository of Otherkind knowledge in the nine worlds?"

Again Cha Fa answered, this time in between licking my ear. "We've already cleared out some things that so improve the flow. She has some good ideas." She half-gestured to a stack of cast-off books.

I pushed my hat back. "She has some hopped up ideas." I picked up a dog-eared paperback with a faded image of a buxom dame on its cover.

"You're getting rid of this?"

Cha Fa slid-walked across the floor. "I want to slip from the clutter holding back my soul the way a snake sheds its skin." She caressed my cheek and bit her lip. "You want to see me in only my clear, uncluttered skin, don't you, lover?"

"Yeah, sure. Along with well over half the population of the planet. But *this* book? This is the Whispers, isn't it?"

She walked behind me, hand slipping from my cheek to bare neck. "So what if it is? It's old."

"Yeah, it's old! So, let me get this straight – you're seriously planning to chuck out the repository of the first words incanted that brought this universe – *all* universes – into existence?"

She shrugged, and her sheer skirt shrugged with her. "I pressed it to my lips. I didn't feel its bliss."

Bong-Cha leaned in between us. "Ah there. Can I ask what the Whispers is? All I see is a blank notebook."

"Yeah, doll. You actually see an ancient tome with words

that, when spoken, can alter the very fabric of existence."

"No, I'm pretty sure I see a blank notebook."

I pulled my hat down. "Yeah, and I'm pretty sure I see an old pulp novel. The Whispers has an adaptation to hide itself – selective recog. It chooses how you remember it. And, since memory is so much of human perception, how we remember it is how we see it." I pushed my hat back. "How did you even know about this place?"

Bong-Cha shrugged and smoothed her skirt. "If you lived a pure, decluttered life, Mr. Wong, you wouldn't leave papers lying around. I want to see how you are – how you move through the world – so I can help you unclutter your hurt soul." She walked over to Cha Fa. "And who better to ask than your lover."

"We're not lovers."

Cha Fa reclined on a Roman-era *chaise lounge* and cupped her head in her hands. "You hurt me, lover."

Bong-Cha looked confused. "She calls you *lover*."

I pulled my hat down. "She calls me a lot of things – most of them not repeatable in polite company." I turned to Cha Fa. "And if we're done talking about interior redecoration, I have a few questions."

Cha Fa sat up. "You only come here when you want something, lover." She leaned back again and opened her legs almost imperceptibly. "And what you want is never me."

I felt my heart in my throat and remembered a time out in the woods behind the library where …

I pushed my hat back. "There's a new player in town. And I know nothing about it. Them. Whatever."

Cha Fa walked over to me and pressed her body to mine. "Ah, but you *do* know, lover. I can see it in your eyes."

"I don't."

She trailed long fingers across my chin and throat. "You do. But you don't remember."

9

I've said it before – memory is a tricky thing. It's made trickier when what you're remembering is a near-immortal fox spirit who ages backwards and seems to remember carnal romps with you that you don't.

But that's just a regular Monday afternoon in my life.

I'd met Leng Cha Fa when I first set up as an exoterric consultant. She slipped into my life like a pulp-novel dame slips into the psyches of anachronistic young boys – all cascading hair and curve-hugging dresses.

"You're the exoterric consultant, right?" she hummed at the front door of my old dingy Chungking Mansions apartment – long before I settled in the back of a bar – as all of Hong Kong bustled with Lunar New Year busy-ment.

I slapped my hat on. "It's exoterric, actually. With two *R*s."

"That's what I said. Exoterric."

"Did you? I mean … right. Yes."

She took a step toward me, and I could feel the warmth of her body through the dank of the concrete corridor. "Is there a problem?"

"Problem? No. It's just. Um. Most people get that wrong."

She ran a long finger down the length of my nose. "Oh, lover. Can't you tell by now that I'm not most people?"

"Um. Yeah. Sure."

Her eyebrows shot up. "Sure? That's all you see?" She stepped back. "Take a *really* good look at me." Hands on hips, hips contrapposto. "Now answer me – do you think that I'm most people?"

I swallowed hard and pushed my hat back. "You're trying to tame me." I pulled my hat over my eyes. "I guess that doesn't make you most people, but I'll tell you, doll, I'm not easily tamed."

Her laughter bounced around in the dull grey hallway. Old Lady Cheng poked her head out the next-door apartment.

"Oh, you're a wildcat, are you, lover?" She stepped close again, and the heat of our bodies mingled like the only two single people at a wedding of people they don't know. "I like that. You and I are going to be great friends." She ran her finger along my nose again, this time continuing on along my lips, chin, throat and down to the third button of my rumpled linen shirt. "Or more than friends?"

I caught air in my throat. “Are you asking?”

She faux-pouted. “I always ask, lover. It’s only polite.” Another step closer, leaning in. “Aren’t you going to invite me in?” her hot breath said in my ear. “I have a case for you.”

Case. The word rang like a temple bell through my cheap-cot-aching joints and edge-of-hungry belly. I pushed my hat back. “Case?”

She sidled by me into my ramen-package-strewn apartment. “You make it sound like this would be your first time.”

I grasped at shreds of my composure. “Why would it be my first time?”

She looked at me like I’d just dribbled chocolate milk on my shirt. “It would be your first time because you haven’t had a case before. Nothing to worry about.” She pressed her heat against my wrinkled linen. “I’ll be gentle.”

Cha Fa flopped onto a corner of my unmade bed, laid back and stretched her arms above her head. I had images of cats. Or foxes.

“Sorry about the mess.” I tossed my hat in a corner. “I don’t get many visitors.”

She propped herself up on her elbows. “Oh yes?” She cast appraising eyes over my wrinkled clothes and deep purple eye bags. “A prime stallion like you? That surprises me, lover.”

“You’re still not going to tame me.”

“I’m not trying.”

I laughed, and it sounded forced.

She stood up. "But enough of this foreplay." Finger down my nose, lips, throat. "As much as I'm enjoying it." Back down on the bed. "The *Nian* is back."

I reached for my hat and, not finding it, scratched the back of my head. "Right. Well. That's … bad."

"Is it?"

"Isn't it? I mean, the Knee-N. Yikes." I scratched my head again. "Excuse me a minute."

I turned from her and, as surreptitiously as I could in a room slightly bigger than a beach blanket, flipped through my Mandarin-English dictionary. "It's awful that the …" I found the entry for *Nian*. "… year? Wait – the year is back?"

Again, she shot me the dribbled-chocolate-milk-on-my-shirt look. "The Chinese word for *year* comes from a monster who, in the depths of winter, sneaks into villages and eats children. That's what's back, lover."

"Yeah, of course. I'm very familiar with the *Nian.*"

She propped herself up on her elbows again. "Because you're an exoterric consultant, master of all things mythical and mysterious."

"Yep, that's why. The *Nian* and I go way back."

"And yet the *Nian* hasn't been seen for more than a century."

"Well. Maybe not *way* back." I reached again for my hat

and scratched my head instead. "We've never *actually* met."

She stood up and pressed herself to me. "Just to check, lover – how many mythical beings *have* you encountered."

"More than you'd expect."

"I'd expect none."

"Well, then more than that."

Finger down my nose, lips, throat. "You're cute." Her hands through her black hair. "But I'm cuter."

"No argument here."

She spun away from me, her body tightening. "How do I know I can trust you?"

"I'm the world's only exoterric consultant. That's got to count for something."

"I suppose it does, lover." Turning back. "Just not enough."

I stepped toward her. "What would convince you?"

She smiled and looped her arms around my neck. "I think we should sleep together and lie around in bed after. That kind of intimacy is the only thing I trust." She shot a look at the unmade folding bed. "But alas, lover, we don't have time. The *Nian* is moving."

When my head stopped spinning, she was already out the door. And I swear I saw a flash of orange fur.

10

Kowloon Walled City was once a Chinese fort that got taken over by squatters once the British moved in. Those who had squatters' rights built dozens of fifteen-storey high-rises in the single city block of space and created a maze of dark, winding streets. Sidestreets were so narrow that a human being would have to walk sideways to pass through. Those ones even the British authorities wouldn't touch.

But the Triads would.

The cacophony of concrete, cables and crime got torn down in the nineties – I would have loved to have seen it in its heyday – and replaced by a quite pleasant park.

But that's not where Cha Fa was taking me. This was no stroll with a dashing dame.

We were going to the old sewers under the park.

It turns out that Kowloon Walled City – and the Chinese

fort before it – stood on that particular ground for a damn good reason.

Because beneath that seven-acre rectangle of land slept the *Nian,* a mythic nasty who devoured the outgoing year. And chomped a few children besides.

At least that's what Cha Fa said. She might have been nuts.

I slipped sideways through two slime-slick pipes and pulled my hat hard over my eyes. "*Yiu!* Why'd this *Nian* choose a dump like this to set up shop? A room at the Peninsula would be way comfier. Plus, room service."

She stalked in front of me, managing the tight space of pipe and cable and dripping black water with a more-than-human grace. "We Otherkind don't choose where we live, lover," she said without turning back. "We are given our allotment, and we tend it with pride for our centuries in this realm."

I pushed my hat back. "And do you have a ... what? An allotment, too?"

"I'm keeper of the Underlibrary."

"The who now?"

I could sense her eye roll without seeing her face. "The Underlibrary is the repository of all mystic knowledge since the birth of the oldest gods. It houses the Whispers itself – the words that brought existence into being." I heard a smile in her words. "But you know that, of course – being the world's only exoterric consultant."

"Oh, you said the *Under*library. I thought you said *wonder* library. Yeah, I know all about the Underlibrary. Want to see my Underlibrary card? Yeah, I know it. The Murmurs and all that."

"The Whispers."

"Yeah, that's the joker. I was just testing you."

"You were testing the keeper of the Underlibrary about the name of the oldest, most powerful book in her collection?"

I reached out and put a teacherly hand on her shoulder. "And you did great, doll."

"Are all of you Foursquares this infuriating?"

I pulled my hat down and jutted out my chin. "Nope. Just me."

"Charming. Poor me."

"Poor you? Nah. You get to spend time with the one and only King Wong."

"You're not the one and only King Wong. There's a dentist in Hung Hom and a realtor in the New Territories, both called King Wong."

"Yeah, but are they as infuriating as me?"

Her body tensed. "I wouldn't know."

"But you've researched people with my name?"

She tensed deeper. "I live in a library. Research is what I do."

I watched her hipsway in that curve-hugging dress through

the slime-slick pipes. “Somehow I doubt that, doll.”

“What?”

“What *what?* I never spoke.”

“Right.” Her body relaxed.

“Right.” I pushed my hat back. “So how long do you get to play librarian?”

“Until a produce an heir. Then I get to leave this ... world.”

“Like … die?”

“If you call being transported to the Jade Palace where my every whim is carried out by oiled young men who don’t speak unless I speak to them *death*.”

“Well. Kinda.” I pushed my hat back further, and with it, thought I’d push my luck, too. “So how’s that producing an heir thing coming along?” Pushing further. “You wouldn’t want help, would you?”

“I believe it’s usually done with help, isn’t it? Even among you Foursquares?”

“Yeah, I suppose.”

“I have a consort. A Frog Prince. A powerful being who ravishes me in his pond.”

“Frog prince? Pond? Sounds unsanitary.”

“Oh, it is, lover. Delightfully unsanitary.”

“So, what’s it like? I mean, his –”

Before I could finish, we pressed into a room untouched by the sewers and water pipes that feed the human condition. No.

Not a room. A *chamber*. The stone walls looked carved not by human hands or slow drips of water or harshness of wind. They looked carved by the passing of time itself – smooth and natural, but with intent and forethought.

And the smell.

Gone was the smell of humanity entirely – the sewer, the stagnant water – and the smell of pure nature, sacred and unholy, assaulted my nostrils. Sage. Ozone. Ancientness.

"Shh," she said without turning. "This is the *Nian*'s lair."

"Hey," I said too loudly, and it echoed off the time-smooth walls. "What does this *Nian* thing look like?" I pulled my hat down. "I want to be prepared when I see it."

She turned. "Oh, lover. You'll know it when you see it." She ran her finger from my lips to my chest. "And you will most definitely *not* be prepared."

A high roar that was half Godzilla, half run-over alley cat ripped through ozone-heavy air.

I shot a look at Cha Fa once I pushed my heart from my throat. "I take it that's Neddy *Nian*." I stood tall and pressed my shoulders back trying to look like an action hero. "How do we deal with it?"

Cha Fa took me by the shoulders with strong hands. "*We* don't deal with it at all. I'm Leng Cha Fa, keeper of the Underlibrary and protector of the Whispers. I could send a *Nian* running back to the old year with a snap of my manicured fingers." She cupped my stubbled chin in her hand. "This one's all for you, lover. It's time you earn your title." She smiled and turned away. "Maybe I'll see you again sometime."

"You bet, doll. I've got that Underlibrary card I've got to use."

But she was gone in a flash of orange fur and smell of primeval forest.

I was glad she didn't tell me what the *Nian* looked like – this was one joker that was better to see in person.

It pounced into the room with the body of a dog and the face of a lion, sporting ox horns down the length of its spine and ice-like fire from its eyes. Again it roared its Godzilla, alley-cat-road-kill roar, and flies erupted from its maw.

In its mouth, I saw rotting remains of what it had devoured.

So, there I was, facing an immortal demon-dog-lion-thing without the help of whatever hopped up immortal had brought me here.

But that's a story for another time. Maybe it'll end up in a book someday.

This wasn't the time to get bogged down in memory.

11

Back in the cool mist of the Underlibrary, Leng Cha Fa pressed the orange fur of her corset against my rumpled shirt and her lips against the stubble on my chin. If I'd forgotten anything about some new baddie threatening my town, this wasn't the way to remember. Pushed up against the bosom of hyper-sexual, possibly immortal fox spirit, I could barely remember my name.

Cha Fa pulled away fast. I heard a giggle from Bong-Cha and shot her a look.

She looked away and smoothed her dress.

Cha Fa trailed her long fingers across my cheek. "Not now, lover." She stretched herself across the *chaise lounge* and cupped her head in her hands. "I need to know who I'm doing this for." She licked her lips and locked me in her dark eyes. "Who's the client?"

I pulled my hat down. "No client. This one's personal."

"Oh, lover – how are you going to afford to buy me nice things if you keep working for free?"

"I can't afford to buy you nice things even *when* I get paid for the work I do."

Bong-Cha snickered again. I let it go.

Cha Fa leaned forward. "Fair point." She leaned deeper and pressed her breasts together. "But seducing me with baubles isn't what you're here for, anyway. It never is." She looked up at me. "You want to know about who – about *what* – is horning in on your beloved Hong Kong."

"You got a lead?"

Cha Fa looked to Bong-Cha and back to me. "Oh, lover. I wish it were that simple."

I pushed my hat back. "Would someone please tell me what's going on with this sorority sister act?"

A sound from the door and we all turned.

A tower of blue flame shot up in the direction of the door. I turned to Cha Fa.

"What?" I said to her terrified face. "What are you looking at? Was it something I said?"

I turned back around to the direction she was looking in and saw again the tower of blue flame.

"*Yiu!* Where'd that come from?"

"It can't be them," Cha Fa whispered. "King – don't look

away," she called to me.

Without taking my eyes off the flame, I stepped beside Bong-Cha. "Don't let it worry you, doll. All a normal Thursday afternoon for me."

"No wonder your life is so cluttered. And it's Monday."

"Oh. In that case, this is really out of the ordinary."

The flame died. I turned to Cha Fa. "What was … what? What were we talking about?"

She reclined on *chaise lounge*. "Oh, lover. Why do you have to be so … *human?*"

"I wouldn't have it any other way, babe." I shot her a smile. "And neither would you."

"You don't remember what we just saw?"

"Saw? All I just saw was you flaunting your goods around the library." I pulled my hat down. "And I see that a lot."

She turned to Bong-Cha. "And you, neither?"

Bong-Cha looked confused. "We were talking. And then. Did something happen?"

Cha Fa stood up and pulled her silk robe around herself. "Humans – useless."

I held out an arm to stop her. "Hey, babe. Sure, I'm useless, but that's no way to talk to the nice, mystical, clean-up lady."

Cha Fa stared me a look that could shatter glass.

I pulled my arm back.

She picked a slim, silk-bound book from a shelf and leafed

through it. "I suppose you'll need something to break the memory wipe." She stopped at a page and smiled. "And there's nothing better than this." She looked at me like a dieting oil company exec looks at a T-bone. "For either of us."

She snapped the book shut but didn't have a chance to cast whatever hopped-up spell she had planned.

The thick wooden door rang with an insistent pounding.

Thung. Thung. Thung.

I looked to Cha Fa. "I think it's for you."

She pulled her robe tighter around herself and faced the door, shoulders and hips square and taut.

"Enter freely and of your own will," she said quietly.

The door swung open. I snaked an arm around Bong-Cha and pulled her to me. "Nothing to worry about, doll. For me, this is just a normal Thursday."

"Right. It's Monday."

"Oh. Then we might have a problem."

Towering over the three of us came the … thingy. I saw something familiar in its blue skin, hooked beak and turtle shell on its back. I thought of Dr. Rodney.

The thing locked me in its black, pinprick eyes.

I took off my hat and shot out a hand. "King Wong, exoterric consultant. How you doing?"

It cocked its bone-crusted head.

I slapped my hat back on. "Not the chatty type, eh? How

about an introduction then? Just name, rank and serial number?"

"I?" the thing said from its beak. "I am an Inheritor of this paltry little place."

"I'd hardly call the Underlibrary *paltry*."

"No, human. I am the Inheritor of this whole meaningless sphere. Inheritor of the Earth itself."

"Oh yeah?" I pushed my hat back. "I guess I need to update my will. I don't remember including you." I pulled my hat down. "Good thing I'm not dying anytime soon, eh, chuckles?"

"What?" The Inheritor snapped its head at me. "Of course you are, human. Along with all your paltry humankind."

"I didn't get that memo."

The Inheritor stretched out its long arms and scraped the book-lined walls of the Underlibrary. "And this shall be my sanctum – a holy refuge of the cast off."

"Think again, chuckles. Leng Cha Fa might have something to say about that. And you're no match for her on a bad day. Cha Fa?" I turned to her, but all I saw was a flash of orange fur and multiple tails.

The Inheritor snapped its head back to me. "You were saying, human?"

I flashed a smile and shot a look at Bong-Cha. "I was just telling my companion here to run."

She looked confused. "What?"

"Run!" I called as the long arm of the Inheritor slashed through the spot where we'd been standing.

It snapped its beak half a dozen times. "Let the purging of the human stain begin – with the fool king, King Wong."

12

Libraries are odd places. The eerie quiet that lies atop all the voices of the dead speaking from closed books is palpable. It gets into your bones.

And it's odder still when the voices in those books are gods and demons from the oldest mists of mythology.

I pulled Bong-Cha behind the stacks, paused then pointed to a wall pinned with character-scrawled pieces of bark.

"Stay low and meet me at the card catalogue," I said, the memory of the Inheritor already fading.

"What's a card catalogue?"

I pushed my hat back. "How young are you?"

"Twenty-three."

"*Yiu!* I have muscle spasms older than that." I looked around. "What were we talking about?"

"Muscle spasms?"

"And why are we hiding on the floor behind a wall of books?"

She furrowed her brow. "Something about whoever was at the door, maybe?"

I stood up. "Okay, this is getting weird. I feel like I've been forgetting something all day."

Her eyes shot behind me. "Forgetting something?" She smiled. "That's the sign of a mind too cluttered." She leaned toward me. "I can help you live a life simple and free."

"I bet you can, doll. I bet you can." The hairs on the back of my neck shot up, and I turned.

Looming over us was a nine-foot-tall, blue skinned man-monster, its beak gaping.

"*Yiu!* Where did you come from, chuckles?"

The Inheritor snapped its head to the side. "King Wong – are you ready for your purge?"

"My purge? That's what happens when you eat the daily recommended intake of fibre, right?"

"I will purge the human stain from this place and inherit my rightful queendom."

"Sorry, sweetheart." I pulled my hat down. "Not while I'm breathing."

"Is that so? Then I will end your breathing, fool king."

The Inheritor reached out an arm to us, crabbed fingers stretching then exploding into detritus – nails, splinters of wood, rusted screws and bent brackets.

I turned and covered Bong-Cha, and the hardware store vomit ripped into my back.

I snapped my head around to see where the attack came from, and saw a nine-foot-tall, blue skinned man-monster.

"*Yiu!* Where did you come from, chuckles?"

The monster's beak smiled – as much as beaks can smile.

"King Wong – you're making this too easy."

Bong-Cha put her hands on my head, stopping me from looking at her.

"Mr. Wong – how did you forget the Inheritor?"

"Forget?" I said without looking at her. "How could I forget this joker?"

"But you did. It was always here."

The beak smiled wider.

"No," I said and glared into the Inheritor's cold blue eyes as Bong-Cha pulled nails and splinters from my back. "That's selective recognition – the Otherkind adaption that makes Foursquares forget what they've seen." I pulled my hat down. "But I'm no ordinary Foursquare – it doesn't work on me."

The Inheritor snapped its head to the side. "More ordinary than you think, King Wong, when in the presence of a being with my power. I will end the fool king."

I stood up. "Chuckles, if I had Star Ferry fare for every cut-rate demon and angry shadow who threatened to end me, I'd head over to Central way more often." I pushed my hat back. "Well. No. I wouldn't. I don't like it there. What I'm trying to say is that jokers like you threaten to end me a lot. Enough that I'd remark on it." I looked up into its cold eyes. "That doesn't sound as tough. Can I start again?"

Waves of hard *déjà vu* crashed over me. I remembered that conversation with the Inheritor, and I remembered remembering it.

Selective recognition.

Yiu.

How much had I forgotten already?

"Too much, lover," Cha Fa's voice said inside my head.

Without noticing, the books were gone, I was in the woods behind the Underlibrary where Cha Fa and I …

A shot of orange fur darted through the undergrowth.

I pushed my hat back. "Cha Fa? What's going on?"

A hand on the back of my neck, and I turned to look into Cha Fa's dark eyes.

She stroked my neck. "You're special, lover. But not special enough. Not for these things. You won't remember them."

"I need to. I'm the only one."

"Maybe it's time to let the Foursquares go. Abandon them to their fate. What have they done for you?"

"Not a lot, doll. But they're still my people."

"Come away with me to the woods and wild. Leave them to this new menace."

I pulled my hat down and felt the pull of her whispered words on more parts of me than I'd care to name. "I can't, doll. They need someone. They need me."

She pulled her hand from my neck. "You're a narcissist. They don't need you. You need to feel special."

"That's a possibility, doll. But, still – a need's a need."

"Kiss me."

"Cha Fa – we've been through this. I can't do that. You know I'm a married man."

"She left. And don't flatter yourself, lover. This isn't about you. It's about selective recognition."

I slit my eyes. "I'm no ordinary Foursquare, doll. Selective recognition doesn't work on me."

She pulled away and put her hands on her hips. "Oh yeah? Then tell me about the Inheritor."

"Inheritor of what?"

"Big blue thing with a turtle shell on its back."

"Never heard of it. I'd remember something like that."

She pressed her lips to my cheek and breathed against me. "Lover – you're here. Right now, you're trapped in the stacks of the Underlibrary at the mercy of a being I've only heard legends of. The Inheritor."

"No."

"You don't remember."

"It's not right. I'm … I don't know where I am."

"You're trapped in the stacks of the Underlibrary at the mercy of the Inheritor."

I pulled her body against mine. "Why don't I know that?"

"The Inheritor is something that Hong Kong has never seen before, lover." She put her face in front of mine. "I can help."

Something old and crabbed softened in me. "Yes. Help me."

"If I do, you can never see me again."

13

The funny thing with Otherkind – well, maybe more terrifying than funny – is that, when you're in their presence, they seem to be the only thing that exists. That plays double when the Otherkind you're in the presence of is a being as ancient and powerful as Leng Cha Fa.

I pushed my hat back. "Then I don't want your help. If you're offering some kind of hopped up, Otherkind blood pact where you help me then need to disappear into the deep dark woods, then I want no part of it."

She ran her finger down my nose to my third button. "You can't do this without me."

"Wrong. I've done other things without you."

She turned away but looked back. "Are you sure about that? How do you know I haven't been watching you this whole time? Helping you along when you stumble or fall behind."

She turned back to me and pressed the fur of her corset against my linen. "Like I did the first time."

"As I recall, the first time you left me to dance the Tiananmen two-step with a mythical dog-lion."

"And as *I* recall, human memory is flawed." She pressed in closer. "What would you be without my push into the realm of Otherkind? A sad, middle-aged man with delusions of mythical beasts on the streets of Hong Kong."

"Some would argue I'm a sad, middle-aged man with delusions of mythical beasts on the streets of Hong Kong even *with* your push."

She looked away but kept her body pressed hard to mine. "I would argue with those who would argue that. And I can be very argumentative. Without my help, you would never have married Mei Hu."

I pulled my hat down. "You didn't tell me – why can't I see you again if you help me?"

"You don't want to know."

"I wouldn't have asked if I didn't."

"Oh, lover. You *really* don't want to know."

"Cha Fa. After what we've been through? You're still going to keep secrets from me?"

She looked back at me. "What have been through?"

"I've seen you, you know."

"Naked? Many have, lover."

"No. I've seen you … as a … as a … fox."

"Oh."

I felt my face flush. "Yeah, *oh*."

She pulled from me. "This is different. I can't tell you."

I threw my shoulders back. "You can, and you will. Now."

She stared glass-shattering death eyes at me. "Trying the stern approach? Do you think that will work with me?"

"Something's got to. So I'm just going to keep throwing spaghetti at the wall until something sticks."

"I'm going to help you, and you're going to let me. Then, you'll never see me again."

I unpent the frustration of Dr. Rodney's death at her. "Why?"

She held me in her gaze for a double handful of heartbeats. "Because helping you is a betrayal of all Otherkind. I'll be taken to the Jade Palace and put to death."

"Put to death for helping me? Why?"

"You don't know yet, do you, lover? I forget human memory only works in one direction." She pulled me close to her again. "You're the greatest enemy Otherkind have ever known."

"I think you've got that wrong, Cha Fa. I'm kind of the greatest protector Otherkind have. Not to brag or anything. It's no big deal. But, you know – I'm really the only one who tries to keep you guys safe."

She shook her head and looked away.

"You can't go," I continued. "They can't kill you. I mean – who's going to look after the Underlibrary?" I tried to look into her eyes. She turned farther away. "Did that frog prince ever give you an heir?"

She looked back at me. I couldn't read what was behind those dark eyes.

"No." She half smiled. "But it wasn't for lack of trying. We tried and tried and tried in his pond." Full smile. "Oh, we tried."

"I get the picture."

"But he never could. Otherkind can only produce heirs when the consort is a true match."

I pushed my hat back. "Frog prince wasn't doing it for you, huh? Couldn't you have found someone else?"

"Oh, lover. How do you live in a mind so small? It must be so cramped having to think like a human. My consort wasn't my match because I was – I *am* – cursed with loving someone else."

"Lucky fella."

"But it's a human." She turned from me. "A stupid, small-minded, bumbling, ridiculous, wonderful human in a dumb hat."

"What?"

"Goodbye, lover." She pressed herself against me again. "If

the next universe is fairer and kinder than this one, maybe we'll meet on the other side."

She held me fast. Red panic ran down my trapped arms. "Cha Fa – what are you doing?"

"End the reign of this Inheritor creature. Then. Well." She looked deep into my eyes. "Then do what you need to do, lover."

"Cha Fa – stop this. I can do this without your help. It doesn't have to be this way."

"It's always been this way."

Her lips came close to mine. I felt her hot breath. She pulled away.

She smiled and closed my eyes with two tender fingers. "Don't think of Mei Hu, lover."

I didn't.

She put a firm hand on the back of my head and kissed me.

But you couldn't really call it a kiss.

It was a dance of welcoming and desire. It was perfect acceptance and perfect wanting – at once totally fulfilling and totally unsatisfying.

And I remembered.

14

Memories came back to be like jabs to the gut. The one-legged beast in Dr. Rodney's hall. The threats of the Inheritor. My terror at not knowing what this new Otherkind was. Each hit me hard, and I crumpled on the forest floor.

Cha Fa stood over me. "Does that feel better, lover?"

"No." I stood up and pulled my hat down. "But at least I remember what's been happening to me. Why this one? Why does its selective recognition work on me?"

"No one knows the ways of gods and demons, lover."

"Not even you?"

She smiled and turned away. "Well …"

She reached out to stroke my cheek. I saw a flash of orange fur, and the woods dissolved again into the stacks of the Underlibrary.

The Inheritor again reached out its hand, ready to fire spare parts at me.

"Don't turn around, Mr. Wong," Bong-Cha called.

I turned around. "It doesn't matter now, doll. I remember."

I turned back to the Inheritor. "That's right, chuckles. You've got nothing on me now. I'm not going to forget you, and soon I'll be able to name you and strip your power from you." I jutted a finger into its blue, tattooed belly. "You're over, pal."

Its beak smiled at me, and it lashed out a long arm that caught me under the jaw and sent me flying into the wall of books behind.

Hot pain seared through my back, and I wasn't sure I could move my left leg.

Bong-Cha hovered over me. "Mr. Wong? I think maybe we cut the big-man threats and run, yes?"

"Yeah, doll. Capital idea."

She pulled me up and supported my limping weight.

I cast a look back at the Inheritor.

Bad move.

The Inheritor shot a shower of nails and splinters – stuff from the cast-off junk it was made from. I twisted my pain-hot body to shield Bong-Cha and felt iron and wood shoot into my soft sides.

"*Yiu*, chuckles! This is my good jacket."

The Inheritor snapped its head to the side. "Of course. The

bumbling hero. More worried about a quip than saving his sorry skin."

"My skin isn't sorry for anything. I moisturize."

The Inheritor stopped and looked at the fallen books scattered on the floor. "But maybe it is not yet time to scrub the human stain that is King Wong. Perhaps that's a task best left to my progeny."

"You never told me you had kids – congrats."

Its beak opened wide and showed off its razor teeth. "Yes. Oh, yes. As a first meal in their new lives, let my progeny feast on the fool king, King Wong.

Bong-Cha pulled at my shoulder. "Mr. Wong? What about that running plan?"

"Still a capital idea, doll."

She pulled me through the high door and out the mouth of the cave.

"Where to?" she said.

"What? I hadn't gotten that far."

"How do we get out of this place?"

I pointed, and the pain in my side pulled my arm back down. "The lift is over there."

"There's nothing over there."

"There has to be."

"There isn't."

I pushed my hat back. "Well how do we get back to

Foursquare land?"

"You're the expert."

"Oh yeah."

"So?"

"So what?"

"How do we get back to Foursquare … whatever you call it. How do we get back to the world?"

The Inheritor ducked through the high doors.

"King Wong." It snapped its head to the side. "I will leave my progeny to devour you. But in the meantime, I have plans for you, fool king."

"Plans? I'll have to check my calendar. I'm a busy guy." I winced at the pain in my side and back. "I'll see if I can fit you in."

The Inheritor leaned down to my face, and I pulled my hat down. "Ever glib, ever the fool king, King Wong." A long tongue licked through the razor teeth in its beak. "But not for much longer. Not when my progeny devour you as their first taste of cleansing the human stain."

And then it was gone with a scraping of wood and metal.

I stared at the spot it stood.

Bong-Cha put a hand on my shoulder. "What are you looking at?"

"What?" I shook the stare from my face. "Just recovering, doll."

“From what?”

I pushed my hat back. “From what? From that big old, turtlebacked meanie who was just threatening my existence.”

“What?” She laughed. “Are you playing some kind of joke on me?”

I thought of Cha Fa’s kiss.

“Selective recog,” I said to no one.

“What?”

“Selective recog. It’s an adaptation most Otherkind have developed. Makes Foursquares forget seeing Otherkind.”

She put her hands to her hips. “That’s not possible. No adaptation can affect the minds of a separate being.”

“Believe what you want. But imagine a race that wants to hide. Rather than adapting speed or teeth or muscles, it adapts to slipping into the shadows.”

“Okay. Maybe.”

“Add to that a culture that has ceased to believe in its own myths. Even if you *think* you saw what you saw, there’s all this hopped up cultural baggage that tells there’s no way ghosts and zombies and whatever exist. You’d convince yourself you only saw a shadow or trick of light.”

“I get it.” She looked up at me with searching eyes. “How do we get rid of it?”

“Get rid of it?”

“Selective recog. I want to remember.”

I turned away. “Cha Fa showed me a way.”

“Good.”

I looked at her. “Yeah?”

“Yes.”

“Okay.” I put a hard hand on the back of her head and pulled her lips close to mine.

She wrenched her head away and slapped me hard. My hat fell to the forest floor.

I rubbed my jaw. “Right. I probably could have explained that better.”

“Maybe. I have no interest in making out with a man who has back spasms older than I am in a mystical, otherworldly forest.”

I moved in closer again. “Cha Fa stripped selective recognition from me with a kiss. I thought the same thing might work for you.”

“Ah yes. Seriously?”

“Worth a shot.”

She leaned closer. I felt her breath against my lips. “This is how you finally find a way to kiss me, Mr. Wong?”

I pulled back. But only a little. “Hey – we’re stuck in the mists of mythology-land with no obvious way out. I need someone beside me who remembers what’s going on.”

“Could you want to a little?”

I smiled. “I’ll do what I can, doll. I’ll do what I can.”

She moved in first, hot breath on the inhale. The gradual firing of nerve endings on lips sparking down in forking paths. The gravitational pull to take more, to pull closer. Desire. Movement. Stillness.

Then a scream from Bong-Cha that split the unearthly silence and shot me back against the hard hulk of a dead tree.

15

I've kissed dames who loved me, and I broke their hearts. I've kissed dames I loved, and who broke my heart. I've kissed dames I couldn't stand, and who couldn't stand me. Mostly those, actually.

I'd never had a dame scream for her life after a kiss.

"What was that thing?" she said after she caught her breath.

I pulled my hat down. "That's the thing, doll – I don't know."

Her eyes went wide. "If not you, then who?"

"If not me there's not a single joker on the face of this sorry, Foursquare planet who would know."

"Ah there. That's bad."

"It's decidedly less than good." I cast my eyes around the forest floor and saw a glimmer of metal. "There's the lift button. Smashed."

"Oh yes. How do we get back up?"

"That's the thing, doll – I don't know."

"If not you –"

"No one, babe. No one." I pushed my hat back. "Let's make that the standard answer every time you ask me that question and be done with it."

"So things are bad."

"Definitely south of the good line."

"Ah there. Have you ever gotten back up another way?"

"I've never needed to. You don't milk a mouse when there's beer in the fridge."

"What?"

"Forget it, doll." The hairs on the back of my neck stood up. "Let's not stand around jawing and give the Inheritor or its kids an easy meal."

"Where should we go?"

"Somewhere where the veil between this world and ours is thin."

"Ah yes. And where would that be?"

"Damned if I know, doll." I took her hand and led her into the woods. "Damned if I know."

The forest was something out of a knock-off painting lazy tourists pick up at the Temple Street night market. Shocks of bamboo rose through a low-hanging mist, and finger-like mountains projected upward in the distance.

A birdcall split the air – high and lonesome and clarion. Bong-Cha snapped her head up to look for the source. I pulled my hat down and smiled.

"*U-wa!*" she said. "Look at that. So simple and free. A real *Bonghwang.*"

The vast bird trailed long feathers behind, casting shimmering air from her body as she flew.

"That may be the Korean word, doll, but don't say that to its face. That's a *Fenghuang.*"

The bird circled back, her tailfeathers curling around her.

"Ah there. What's she doing?"

"Hunting. *Fenghuang* snatch up the nastier of the mythic nasties."

Bong-Cha looked at me. "How can a being of such beauty keep its purity if it clutters itself by eating the impure?"

"No one said anything about eating, doll. This is the world of myth, not the world of nature. For all I know, the *Fenghuang* here lives on rainbows and love juice." I pushed my hat back. "She doesn't eat the baddies. She just gets rid of them."

"She's beautiful."

I squinted at the circling wings overhead. "Watch your step, though. Whatever she's hunting is close." I swung out in front of Bong-Cha. "Let me lead the way."

"Oh yes."

"Pretty mind-blowing, eh? All this mythological stuff? But

you're handling it pretty well. Better than most. You've got a good head on you, doll."

"Ah there. What makes you think it's my first time?"

"Is it?"

"My first time? You tell me. You're more experienced than I. How am I doing?"

"Admirably, doll. You're doing admirably." I pulled my hat down. "Tell me about the others. I mean – tell me about your other encounters with Otherkind."

"Are you sure? That won't make you jealous?"

"I'm tougher than I look."

"When I was little, I saw –"

In a flapping of feathers, Bong-Cha screamed long and high.

I spun around to see the *Fenghuang* swoop down on wind-ripping wings, talons cutting space right at Bong-Cha.

I leapt at them and was cast to the dust by a wing for my trouble.

Grabbing at anything, my left hand caught an ankle and my right caught one the bird's seven tailfeathers. Before I could orient myself to which way I wanted to yank, I was lifted off the ground into the mists above.

I held fast to a feather, my eyes on Bong-Cha wrapped in the bird's talon.

"Hang on, doll," I called to her. "I've got this one."

“Ah there,” her tone was calm and even. “I have no doubt that you believe that. I’m afraid the facts of this situation might argue otherwise.”

I pulled at the tailfeather, hand over hand, and inched closer to Bong-Cha. “Nah, I go this one, doll.”

From behind me, three of the other tailfeathers curled and twisted like a psychedelic poster around my legs and right arm.

Bong-Cha’s tone had lost in cool, evenness. “Mr. Wong? I could use some of your overconfidence now.”

“No problem,” I spat out as a fourth tailfeather wrapped around my throat. “I got this –” bright red feathers choked my words “ – one!”

I’d get to her. No way was I going to allow a *Fenghuang* to spirit off yet another acquaintance of mine. Not again.

A fifth tailfeather joined its compatriot around my throat, and air became scarce.

“Mr. Wong?” Bong-Cha called.

I gasped out a gurgling as the sky turned black and my body went limp. I felt a slight sensation of falling, then only blissful blackness.

16

Defeated, dusty and damned sure I was ready for a win or two today, I pulled myself from the dirt and slapped my hat on. All doors back to my Hong Kong – and the rest of the mortal world – may be gone, but that wasn't going to stop me.

Well, odds are it *was* going to stop me, but I wasn't going to let that thought creep into my aching head.

"Right," I said to no one. "Rescue the decluttering diva or find a way back first?"

I looked to the sky. It was as clear and empty as a used car salesman's smile. "She's a tough dame. I'll find a way home and come back for her." I pulled my hat down and walked toward the Underlibrary, pulling nails and splinters from my bloodied side, and really hoping the Inheritor had gone to play doting mommy to its offspring.

"I guess that only leaves the question of *how* I'm going to get back." I cast my eyes to the twelve-foot-high guardian statues – rippling, muscled men with angry faces or the heads of demons, brandishing their long staffs with broad shoulders and spread legs, lit by the flickering of eternal torches – that flanked the high doors to the Underlibrary. "Any suggestions, chuckles?"

I heard whispers on the cool air.

"Say again? Could whatever spooky, disembodied immortal spirit out there please speak up?" I pushed my hat back. "And maybe enunciate a bit?"

Whispers.

I kicked at the stone floor of the Underlibrary. "Just my luck. I get supernatural help to escape mythical, tourist-painting land, and I can't hear a darn thing."

Whispers.

I ran my fingers idly along books, scrolls and folios stacked on the high shelves. Maybe something here would give me a lead.

Whispers.

I spun around and shouted at the empty air. "I get it, okay? You're toying with me. You're making me think there's something you're saying that I'll never get. Great joke. Very funny. Love it." I pulled my hat down. "You can cut it out, now."

My eye caught the stack of ancient, magical tomes Cha Fa

was planning to donate to the Salvation Army.

Whispers.

I looked at the dog-eared paperback with a faded image of a buxom dame on its cover.

Whispers.

"Oh. Right." I pushed my hat back and addressed the air. "Does that really seem like a good idea? I mean, I've had some bad luck dealing with all this hopped up, magical stuff. Do we really think I should be the one to open a book that can rewrite existence as a whole?"

Whispers.

I shrugged and pushed my hat back farther. "Fine. You're the boss, disembodied whisper voice."

I grabbed the book. It was heavier than it should have been.

A deep purple dread seeped from my hands into the depths of my chest.

"This can't be a good idea."

Whispers.

The book snapped open and thousands of pages where there had only been a couple hundred flapped in an unfelt wind.

Whispers.

"No. I think I'm just going to put this down."

Whispers.

I stooped, the book heavy in my hands.

But I couldn't let go.

"Um, disembodied whisper voice? Is this supposed to happen?"

In place of the whispers came a hundred billion voices at the same time, yet each as clear as a lover whispering in my ear. Every hope, dream and unanswered prayer from every human, Otherkind and whatever else that had ever existed echoed in my all-too-mortal skull.

"Whisper voice? You still there?"

But I couldn't hear my own words. I heard a prayer for rain from a farmer in an unrecognizable land. I heard a lover tell her dreams to someone unworthy of hearing them. I heard a newborn baby howling at a night that wouldn't end.

I looked down at the book, seeing it not as a pulp novel, but as it truly was – brighter than the sun and scrawled in twisting, spiralling letters and words from every language on Earth and some from Elsewhere.

Those letters seeped from luminescent pages into the skin of my hands, up through my linen sleeves. I could feel my heart and lungs fill with unspoken words – words waiting to be breathed into existence, and, with breath, recreate that existence.

The full weight of what I'd done in opening this cast-off paperback hit me like I'd just put the fate of the universe itself at risk.

Because I had.

This was the Whispers – a record of the words spoken at the first moment of creation. Words that *were* creation. Words that, spoken differently – or maybe even by a different voice – would create new unrecognizable universes, tearing down everything that was.

I felt the words heavy in my lungs, wanting – demanding – to be spoken. I felt the raw power of creation ready to explode from my voice and destroy all any of us had ever known.

My jaw clenched – no way I was going to be responsible for destroying all of creation. No way I was going to give all my teachers the satisfaction of saying *I told you so.*

But the words bubbled in my breath. I could feel it – the next time I breathed out, I would create a new universe and rip apart this one.

A second later I felt fine.

I looked at my hands. No letters snaked my skin.

And the buxom dame on the cover was back.

But I wasn't in the Underlibrary.

This place was all light – gold and white and sunshiny, with licks of mist lapping at my ankles.

"Welcome, King Wong," a voice said from everywhere, so nowhere discernible. "Welcome to the Jade Palace."

I pulled my hat down.

A luminescent figure shone brighter than everything else shone – which was already impossibly bright – with a face both ancient and eternally youthful. “Perhaps we can put down the words of creation and leave this universe intact for the time being.”

I dropped the book. “Whatever you say, chuckles.” I pushed my hat back. “Wait – where did you say we were?”

“We’re in the Jade Palace, King Wong.”

“Jade Palace, huh? Then that makes you ...”

His answer came on a long breath. “Yes.”

17

With the life I've led – like being married to an immortal fox spirit – you'd think standing toe-to-toe with the glowing granddaddy of gods and mortals encircled by ancient mists would be just a regular Friday evening. But in truth, I'd only ever seen the Jade Emperor once – that would have been at my wedding reception before Mei Hu …

I thought then he was kind of a jerk.

"My apologies, King Wong. Does my celestial form unnerve your human sensibilities?"

Still a jerk. I pulled my hat down to shield my eyes. "Wear whatever makes you comfortable, *pang yau*."

"Let me adopt the form of a being more suited to worship by human perception."

Air twisted around him, and he changed. Well, he didn't so much change as I felt my eyeballs twist and alter in my skull.

Standing in front of me was a stereotype right out of a Mainland Kung Fu movie – long moustache, longer silk robes and an air of holier-than-thou. I bet whatever form this joker took, he'd still be a jerk.

"Sorry, pal." I pushed my hat back. "It's going to be hard for me to keep a straight face with you in that get up."

"Ah, I see. You don't worship in the traditional way for one of your kind."

"That's an understatement, chuckles."

He reached out to me and did a damn fine impression of modern interpretive dance. "Then, please, allow me to look into your soul and find a form you truly worship."

"Do you really want to poke around in there? You may not like what you find."

But his interpretative dance hands were already searching my soul for something I worship. It kind of tickled. Like putting your hand in warm water you expected to be cold.

Again my eyes bent and changed. Standing in front of me now was a slightly below average height, middle aged Asian man in a rumpled linen suit and a ridiculously anachronistic hat.

Wait.

I was standing in front of myself.

The Jade Emperor looked down at his new body. "Oh dear. This will never do."

"It works for me, pal."

He locked with my own eyes. "Does it, King Wong? Does it?"

Still a jerk.

Again his dance hands reached out to me, and again my eyes bent and refocussed.

"Dr. Rodney?"

In front of me now was a shock of wild white hair and, beneath that, the unusually calm face of Dr. Rodney Lau.

"Does this form suit your human needs, King Wong?"

I pulled my hat down. "Look, chuckles – I'm getting mighty sick of every joker in this story looking down on me because I happened to be born human. Sure, I'm only a half-step up from throwing my own faeces, but it seems pretty unclassy to drawn attention to it."

"This story, you say?"

"Did I?" I pushed my hat back.

"You could have the power to change it." He stepped toward me. "You could have the power to rewrite this cosmos, so your precious humanity stood at the pinnacle of creation." Another step. "Isn't that what you desire? Isn't that why you opened the Whispers – to reform this universe and all the others in your own image?"

"You don't know me that well, pal. Why would I want to live in a world I created? I don't even like using the bathroom after myself."

"You jibe and you jest. But where is the real King Wong beneath the jokes?"

"What if the real King Wong *is* the jokes? Maybe all I am is the words that make me."

He took a step back. "Then that is a fitting sentence for your crimes."

"Crimes? Is this about that overdue library book?"

"You have opened the Whispers – record of the first words spoken that brought this universe into existence. These are words to be spoken by gods, not the lowly likes of you."

"There we go again with the anti-humanism." I pulled my hat down. "And no – I have absolutely no desire to change one speck of existence. Well. Except that I need to be back in the land of the living and not in some hopped up, mythical library."

"An easy task." He smiled. "If one knows how to read the Whispers."

I pushed my hat back. "And if one doesn't?"

His smile darkened. "One accidental pronunciation could create a world unrecognizable to you. One dropped word could blink you out of existence."

"Hm. That's less than good."

He stepped forward and pulled at his shock of white hair. "I can offer you another way."

"Capital, chuckles. Let's do that."

“Excellent.” Another step. “And, as I expected, you agreed without hearing the terms I offer.”

I pulled my hat down. “Yeah, I do that. It’s my one flaw.”

“Aside from being a flagrant egoist.”

“Aside from that.”

“And being a caveman of a sexist.”

“And that.”

“And your complete and utter disregard for the norms of polite society.”

“Meh. Is that really a flaw?”

“Yes.”

“Then that, too.”

“And –”

“I’m going to stop you there and ask about these terms mentioned.” Jerk was enjoying this.

“Of course.” He pulled at Dr. Rodney’s hair. “I will spirit you back to the place and time where you left your world.”

“Capital. I’m in.”

“I haven’t finished.”

I pushed my hat back. “Go on. Don’t let me stop you.”

I saw what looked like a flash of irritation cross his wrinkled face. “However, you must be pure and noble of motive. If you have no intention – and never had any intention – of using the Whispers to remake existence in your image, your safe passage is assured.”

"And if not?"

He smiled, all irritation gone. "If not, then I will cast you into the depths of *Diyu*, there to be tortured until your death."

"That's not great."

He shot me another smile. "I haven't finished. There to be tortured until your death – at which point you will be returned to your original state to be tortured in new and inventive ways until your next death."

"Less great."

"At which point, you will be returned to your original state to be tortured in new –"

"Okay, chuckles. I get the picture."

He pulled at his hair. "Excellent, King Wong. Shall we begin?"

"How are you going to know if my motives are – what did you say? – pure and noble?"

"I won't."

"Oh. You're just going take my word for it, then?"

His smile darkened, and he snapped Dr. Rodney's dry, cracked fingers. "*I* won't know, King Wong. But the *Xiezhi* will."

Bounding up beside him like an infernal Rover came a beast with a dog body, tusked monkey face and pig nose trailing licks of yellow flame. Its head was crowned with horns of bone, with one jutting upward equal to the length of its whole body.

On that horn was a century's worth of crusted blood.

The Jade Emperor pulled at Dr. Rodney's hair. "The *Xiezhi* can discern your guilt on each whiff of wind from your feeble, human mouth." His smile darkened further. "If, after looking at three instances of your life, the *Xiezhi* determines you had intent two of the three times to use the Whispers to remake this universe in your image …"

"Let me guess. I get impaled on that big horn?"

"Exactly, King Wong."

"Capital."

"But, King Wong – you didn't ask where the *Xiezhi* would impale you."

I pulled my hat down. "Do I want to know?"

"Oh, no."

The *Xiezhi* sat imperiously on its hind legs, its pig nose twitching as it sniffed the air.

18

With the life I've led, you'd think being put on trial to take a microscope to my faults would be just a regular Saturday morning. Sure, there may have been a couple old girlfriends who read me a laundry list of character defects, but never quite so formally as now, with the Jade Emperor, Holy King of Heaven, sitting on high watching me with an old friend's face and the horny-headed *Xiezhi* sniffing my breath for signs of guilt or lies.

The Jade Emperor pulled at Dr. Rodney's hair. "As I said, King Wong – we will examine three moments from your miserable human life. If my *Xiezhi* detects any intent or desire to now change two or threes of those moments – to use the Whispers to remake the universe to your will …"

"Yeah, yeah. Tortured to death. Brought back to life. Tortured again."

He smiled. “In new and inventive ways.”

I pulled my hat over my eyes. “I hadn’t forgotten, chuckles.”

“Excellent. Then let’s begin.”

The mists that tangled their way through the halls of the Jade Palace coalesced into sunset clouds, light and shadow and colour shifting and blending until images formed. I watched magenta clouds curl and twist into my own younger face.

And the snarling, tusked dog-lion face of the *Nian.*

Then a voice. My voice. Narrating the scene as if through some interior monologue.

I was glad she didn’t tell me what the Nian looked like – this was one joker that was better to see in person.

“Hey there, chuckles,” I said to the Jade Emperor. The sunset video paused. “How did you get this? It’s like you recorded my very thoughts.

“It *is* that we record your very thoughts.”

“All of them.”

“Most definitely.”

The *Xiezhi* sniffed at me.

“Capital.” I pushed my hat back. “Capital.”

“May we continue?”

“With this scene? Sure, let’s stick with this.”

It pounced into the room with the body of a dog and the face of a lion, sporting ox horns down the length of its spine and ice-like fire from its eyes. Again it roared its Godzilla, alley-cat-road-kill roar, and flies erupted from its maw.

In its mouth, I saw rotting remains of what it had devoured.

So, there I was, facing an immortal demon-dog-lion-thing without the help of whatever hopped up immortal had brought me here.

And then I ran.

I ran like a kid whose underwear had just been wedgied up by big kids to where no one would ever find it.

His Jade-ness stepped forward, dissolving the mist movie. He spoke not to me, but to the *Xiezhi*. "You see how King Wong would dare to use the Whispers to remake his life into something less … embarrassing."

I pulled my hat down. "Hey, chuckles – I went back there. I put the *Nian* back in its cage. I earned my title of exoterric consultant."

He pulled at his white hair. "With help from the keeper of the Underlibrary."

"Yeah with help." I was shouting now, spittle flying as I spoke. "Help is what it means to be human." The words surprised me as I spoke them. "Help is what we do – it's how we get things done."

The Jade Jerk seemed pleased I'd resorted to shouting.

"*Xiezhi?*" he said. "What say you?"

The *Xiezhi* sniffed at the dispersed mists that had made up the little movie of my life. It hung its head.

His Jade-ness lost his smile. "*Xiezhi* says this one is inconclusive." He spun away from me. "We move on."

Again sunset mists coalesced into a scene. Again I heard my own interior voice narrating it.

Dr. Rodney was splayed out behind the desk, hands still in the wires of his white hair. Even face-down, I could see the terror in his pale body. His tense legs and arched back showed me he died in primal, human fear of something beyond his comprehension. Visions of blue flames, of turtles and of beaks shot across my brain and were gone.

I took off my linen jacket, covered him with it and slipped back out into the hall.

Bong-Cha smoothed her dress and looked up at me.

"Dead, doll." I ran finger and thumb across my eyes.

"I'm so sorry." She looked away. "Would an embrace ease your pain?"

"What?" I took my hat off and scratched my head.

She swallowed hard. "I'm asking if you need ... a hug."

I slapped my hat down on my head and shot my eyes to her. "No. A hug won't do it this time."

"I wouldn't think so."

"And what would you think?" I said through the catch in my throat.

"You want to find out what did this to him."

I looked away. "I should have been here. I shouldn't have left."

"Should is a word that only serves to clutter our souls with toxic expectations and false boundaries. You were doing what you thought best. You were helping a friend."

"Fat lot of good it did."

She smoothed her dress and said nothing.

Instead, she put her arms around my shoulders and pressed me to her as I fought back the sobs that threatened to shake me open in the sleek steel and glass of the bare hallway.

His Holy Green-ness stepped forward, dissolving again the mists. "You see, *Xiezhi?* To restore the life of his friend – the only one he worships save himself, which is why I wear this form – he would incant the Whispers and remake the cosmos."

He had me there. There's very little I wouldn't do to bring Dr. Rodney back. And, if I had a chance to bring him back … healthy? There's even less I wouldn't do.

I shot a sidelong look to the *Xiezhi*, knowing it could smell my thoughts on my breath.

Jade-y looked even more pleased. "*Xiezhi?*" he said. "What say you?"

The *Xiezhi* sniffed again at the mists, sometimes cocking its head toward me, sometimes to Jade Jerk.

I could feel its deliberation hanging on the misty air, and that didn't help me sweating like a conspirator in court. *Xiezhi* came to me, sniffed long and hard, then looked to the Jade Emperor.

"Ha-ha!" Jade Jerk spouted. "Proof that you would use the Whispers for your own gain."

I pulled my hat down. "Fair enough, chuckles. But we've got one scene left to play."

He smiled. "Oh, yes. We certainly do." His smile darkened. "And you'll love it."

Yet again sunset mists coalesced into a scene.

I saw my wife.

Mei Hu was dressed in the blue silk *cheongsam* I'd gotten her on our honeymoon to the Mainland.

It was what she was wearing the last time I saw her.

The Jade Emperor stepped toward me. "Let's see how this event in your useless, human life colours your guilt."

19

As if watching cloud-rendered footage of my lost wife in the hallways of the Jade Palace wasn't surreal enough, listening to my own voice interior monologuing everything that happened pushed it well into absurd.

I pushed my hat back. "Mei Hu – you don't have to go."

She looked at me half with affection, half with pity. "Oh, sweetie. You don't get it yet, do you? Of course I have to go."

"No. There's a little thing called free will. Heard of it? We could run off somewhere – leave this lousy world behind."

"Lousy world? This is the forest of the gods."

"Meh. Give me pavement and the stink of diesel exhaust any day."

She moved closer but seemed farther away. "I'm not like you, sweetie."

"Don't like diesel exhaust? We'll get an apartment in a

high-rise then. Clean air."

She tried not to smile. "I'm not like you with free will. It doesn't work that way for me. When my people call, I need to go."

"I get it." I pulled my hat down. "Because you have this misplaced sense of duty."

She turned from me. "It's not a sense of duty, sweetie. It's more than that. It's physical. It's ... spiritual."

"Fine. So some spiritual force is telling you to flee deep into some magical forest where I can't go. Can you explain why? I deserve that much."

She moved closer. "King. We've been through this. Don't."

"Yeah, we've been through it." I pulled away. "But I don't get it. So why don't you explain it one more time."

She cast her eyes down. "Like I said – how many times? – my people have sensed the end of our kind coming. They want us all to be safe."

I pushed my hat back and turned from her. "See, that's what I don't get. If their end is coming anyway, why not live a little?"

She sighed a sigh that had been building since we started this argument days ago. "Because I don't have free will."

I pulled my hat over my eyes. "Maybe you should get some."

A high pitched bark-scream shot through the air. When I

turned, Mei Hu was walking toward a muscle-y guy in an orange fur loincloth.

I pushed my hat back. "Oh great. And you're going with him?"

"Sweetie – I'll come back for you when whatever this threat is to my people has passed."

"You won't."

But they were already gone into the underbrush in a flash of fur.

The Jade Emperor stepped forward, dissolving again the mist movie.

I pushed my hat back. "Don't stop it now, chuckles. It was just getting interesting. That fur-loinclothed muscleman didn't even get any lines."

He pulled at Dr. Rodney's white hair. "You know fully well what happened next, King Wong. You left the forest of the gods to wander the human world, a broken man."

"I wouldn't say *broken*. A little bent maybe – but aren't we all?"

He stamped his foot on the polished jade, and for an instant the image of Dr. Rodney dissolved into the being of pure light. "Enough of these quips! You are on trial for your life."

"What better time to keep the tone light?" I turned to the *Xiezhi*. "Am I right?"

It sniffed.

“That’s what I thought.” I pulled my hat down. “Now, chuckles – the burden of proof is on you. How does Mei Hu … leaving prove in any way that I’d want to use the Whispers to give creation an extreme makeover?”

He pulled at his hair. “You would do anything to bring her back.”

“I haven’t done a single thing to get her back yet. She chose to leave. I’m no stalker. I have a very high opinion of women, despite all appearances. And … um … actions.”

“You have done nothing because there is nothing in your human power to do.”

I pulled my hat over my eyes and cocked my head back to look at him. “That’s one way of looking at it.”

He smiled his darkest smile. “Then give me another way, King Wong. Defend yourself.”

The *Xiezhi* sniffed at me and tossed around its horned head. A crust of dried blood from whatever joker was last in my place fell to the polished jade.

“I’m not one to talk about my lovers without them present.”

A belch of laughter erupted from the Jade Jerk, and I swore I heard some of the real Dr. Rodney in it.

“You have done little else but talk of Mei Hu since she left you to be with her own kind. Despite everyone telling you of her death.” His smile darkened further. “Shall I bring the mist again to show you?”

I shuddered. Hearing my own inner monologue played back at me was worse than hearing my voice on tape. "No, need, your royal Jade-ness. You're absolutely right – there's little else I do."

"So? Give us your defense."

The *Xiezhi* sniffed at the fallen scab of blood. Then at me.

I pushed my hat back. "Okie-dokie." I cupped my chin in my hand in my best lawyer look. "The way I see it, is that I wouldn't *want* to bring Mei Hu back, even if I had the chance."

Impatience flashed across Jade Jerk's face. "Yes, that's what you're trying to prove. The *Xiezhi* and I wish to know *why*."

"I'm getting to that your holy green-itude." Okay. Stalling for time while I came up with an idea wasn't going to work. "I'm getting to that." I'd just have to start talking and see what came out. As usual.

He pulled at his hair. "Well?"

"The way I see it is that so much of my persona – and what a fetching persona it is – is tied up in being this downcast, broken-hearted, romantic hero type. Right?"

"That describes your ridiculous self-indulgence adequately, yes."

I took my hat off and fanned myself with it. "So, think about it – what would happen if I rewrote this universe to bring Mei Hu back to me?"

"You would have your heart's desire. What every human wants." His dark smile. "Is that the best you can do?"

"That's right. I'd be happy." I slapped my hat back on. "But don't think humans *really* want their hearts' desires. For most of us, that's a fate worse than ... worse than the fate you've got planned for me if that *Xiezhi* sniffs a whiff of guilt on my breath." I pulled my hat down. "You see, if I got Mei Hu back, I'd be *happy*. But, because I've invested so much of myself into *not* being happy, if I got happy, I'd cease to be me." Even I was starting to believe myself.

He pulled at his hair. "Perhaps. How does this absolve you of wanting to remake the universe according to your desires?"

I pushed my hat back and leaned toward him. "That's the thing – I would only remake the universe to bring Mei Hu back. But, bringing Mei Hu back would be in conflict with my desires because it would negate my sense of self. If I remade the universe, I wouldn't be me." I pulled my hat down in triumph. "So there wouldn't be a *me* to remake the universe." I resisted tossing off a *checkmate. "Xiezhi* – what say you?"

Jack Jade-jeans looked ready to speak, but the *Xiezhi's* snarl silenced him. It came to me, sniffing around my ankles. And more intimate places.

"If I remake the cosmos, I get what I want."

Sniff.

"If I get what I want, there's no me."

Sniff. Sniff sniff.

“If there’s no me, there’s no one to remake the cosmos.”

Sniff sniff.

“Signed, sealed, delivered.”

20

There was no sense of falling. Or rising. There was no sense of movement at all. In my perception, one second I was in the Jade Palace looking at Dr. Rodney's shock of white hair while the *Xiezhi* nuzzled my nethers, the next I was standing with Bong-Cha and the discount cosmetics shop girl.

Shop girl stared blankly into her phone. "I'm sorry, sir. Lady Leng isn't responding."

I pulled my hat down. "No, I wouldn't expect her to. Not now." I grabbed Bong-Cha's wrist. "Come on." I pulled her from the store and blinking shopgirl.

"Ah there. Where are we going?"

"Somewhere." I threaded through crowds on Nathan Road. "Fast."

"Oh yes. Do you have a plan?"

"One will come to me. Always does." I stopped and turned

to her. "Hey – you were just in the talons of a *Fenghuang* then magically transported back to the world without knowing why." I pushed my hat back. "I expect more ... bewilderment. Awe. Something."

"Expectations are clutter upon our perceptions, obscuring our life simple and free."

"Quite possibly, doll. Quite possibly. But what gives?" I watched a limping old man fiddle with a torn backpack. "Where's the awe and bewilderment?"

The old man tossed his backpack into a rubbish bin.

"Ah there," Bong-Cha said. "As I was trying to tell you. When I was little, I saw –"

From the overflowing rubbish bin, the torn backpack erupted, spewing egg waffle wrappers and coffee cups. But the backpack was … different. The opening had grown teeth and was ravenously chomping at anything that passed by.

Mostly people.

"Get behind me," I barked at Bong-Cha. "I have experience with this kind of thing."

"With sentient backpacks trying to eat passers by?"

I pulled my hat down. "Yeah. More or less."

In a motion, I lunged for the thing with arms spread, hoping to snap shut its zippered maw.

Instead, it saw me coming – with unseen eyes – and bolted. But not before I was able to get my right arm entangled in one of its straps.

That was the day I learned that living backpacks have a remarkable amount of bounding power. The thing bounced through Nathan Road's crowds, dragging me along the filthy pavement with so much force my hat blew off my head.

"Little help here," I called to a wide-eyed cop. Nothing. If I paid taxes, I'd be more than a little upset.

And Barney Backpack wasn't about to stop for the crowds huddled to cross Austin Road. In a leap, it bounded over the knot of pedestrians with my rag-doll body still in tow.

But even a sentient backpack's bounding power has limits. At the peak of its arc, it lost momentum, just as I pulled my arms free from its straps.

Falling, and with terror across its zippered backpack mouth, it collided bodily with a careening garbage truck.

I fell into hard, strong arms. I looked up into the face of the triad-tattooed gym rat from earlier that day. "Much obliged, pal," I said and reached for my missing hat.

He plonked me on the ground. "Don't I know you?"

I flashed my best grin, which wasn't that great even when I hadn't been dragged three blocks by a backpack. "Seems unlikely."

From the distant garbage truck, I watched arms, hands, claws and eyes struggle to escape from the compactor. Cast off things trying to be free. I lost myself in the crowd as the light turned and they crossed Austin.

"What was that?" Bong-Cha said as she plopped my hat back on my head.

"That? Just a living backpack. With a remarkable amount of bounding power."

"Ah there. I mean what manner of Otherkind was that?"

I pushed my hat back. "That's the thing, doll. I don't know."

"But if not you …?"

"Yeah, we've been through this. If not, me – no one." I pulled my hat over my eyes. "And if I can't name them, I can't stop them."

"Ah there."

"You said it, doll. All I know is that discarded household items are coming to life and attacking their former owners."

"Of course," she shot out. A couple people turned and stared.

I pushed my hat back. "You're telling me you know what kind of mythical baddie this is?"

"Oh no. But I know where we can start."

"Oh yeah?"

"I have a client – an avid collector. Some would say hoarder. He collects – *collected* – comic books, records, commemorative spoons. The usual things. I'm decluttering his life, so his soul can find its true purpose."

"How much decluttering are we talking?"

"He's hired a private transport company to haul it away. They arrive this afternoon."

"Sounds like a good place to get some more details on these cast-off critters. Where does this soul-cluttered hoarder live?"

"The Peak."

"I knew you were going to say that."

She hailed a cab with her slender arm. We got in and sat in silence.

She took my hand.

"Tell me about her," Bong-Cha said.

"Who?"

"The one who hurt you into toughness."

"No one hurts me, doll."

"Ah there. Not anymore. Not after *she* hurt you." She turned to me. "Or he?"

I thought of Mei Hu. "Look, doll – what makes you think I want to talk about this at all, let alone to some hopped-up, total-stranger, lifestyle-coach dame?"

"If you declutter your memories, they will cease to cause you pain. Oh yes."

I furrowed my brow. "I like my memories just how they are."

Her long fingers stroked my forehead. "No. No, you don't. Why do you live this way?"

"Because the rent's cheap and you can't beat the hours." I

looked out the window to the tunnel traffic.

"Ah there. Always a glib defence."

"You got it, doll."

"And each one-liner cast off into the clutter of your mind." She reached for my other hand. I shoved it in my pocket. "Let me free your burden. Let me clean you."

"No thanks, doll. If I get dirty, there's a Mainland girl at a bathhouse on Ning Po Street I'm sweet on. She cleans me up just fine."

"Ah there. Another one-liner cast off into the clutter."

We pulled up to a swanky, colonial-era house that looked like it had bathrooms bigger than the house I grew up in.

21

The Peak. Just those words are enough to haunt me with images of dinner parties, polo shirts and society women two drinks past what they can hold. Banned to Hong Kong Chinese for most of the colonial era, British settled the Peak to escape the sticky heat of lower altitudes. It's integrated now, but it kept its snooty heritage intact.

Though you can't beat the view.

I turned my collar up against the chill. "This is the place?"

Bong-Cha pulled a silk rope that rang a resounding bell inside. "Oh yes." She gestured to a small mountain of black garbage bags in the driveway. "A small sample of this poor man's clutter."

"I wouldn't call him poor if he lives in a joint like this." I took my hat off, maybe in mute tribute to the passing of such a staggering amount of junk. "Tell me about how you know

Otherkind."

"When I was little, I saw –"

"Wait," I cut her off. "Something's not right." I sidled beside her and pushed the gate. It swung open.

I put my hat back on and pulled it down. "Not like a fat cat like this to leave his security gate open."

"Ah there. An oversight, perhaps?"

I pointed to three security cameras all pointed at the entrance to catch different angles of any would-be intruders. "This joker's got three cameras trained on his front door but he forgets to close it? Not likely." I slid past her through the gate. "Something's not right. Stay behind me."

She strode up the stone steps. "Oh no. This is my client. If something's wrong, I'll be the one who puts it right."

We both tried to push past the other, and ended up walking shoulder-to-shoulder up the steps and through the front door.

Heck yes, something was wrong.

Fat cat's body lay dead on the cold marble floor, shot through with nails and bits of wood.

Above his corpse stood the turtle-shelled, eagle-beaked form of the Inheritor.

It snapped a look at us. "Ah, the fool king returns. You escaped the Underlibrary."

I pushed my hat back and gestured to fat cat's body. "I take it this is your doing?"

"Not my doing, fool king. I am merely here to clean up the mess. This mere human was brought to his end by my mistress."

"Mistress? Kids *and* a mistress, huh? You've got your hands full."

Bong-Cha put a hand on my shoulder. "Mr. Wong. I've been trying to tell you. When I was little, I saw –"

"Now's not the time for walks down memory lane, doll. I'm dealing with a mythical baddie who wants to take over the world."

The Inheritor snapped its beak at me. "No, fool king. I *have* taken over the world. Everywhere and every day, the vast output of Mainland Chinese factories is tossed, discarded and cast off. Everywhere and every day my progeny spring to life in my service." It turned its lizard eyes to Bong-Cha. "And the service of my mistress."

Now I looked at Bong-Cha. "Do you two know each each other?"

She squeezed my shoulder. "Ah there. As I was saying – when I was little, I saw the true power of decluttering, making life simple and free. Oh yes."

I pulled my hat down. "What does that have to do with chuckles here?"

She squeezed my shoulder tighter. "The true power of decluttering comes not from breathing more freely or of a burden lifted from one's soul." Tighter still. "The true power of decluttering comes from the hordes of disembodied Otherkind waiting to inhabit the husks of those cast-off objects."

"Like that hopped up umbrella I was after last night."

"Ah there. Japan's *Kasa-obake.* A being who's one true wish is for corporeal existence, and yet who will only reach for that existence in the form of umbrellas."

I pulled my shoulder from her grasp and turned to her. "When you were little – what did you see?"

She smiled a smile darker than I'd seen on any Otherkind. And she was just a Foursquare human.

"When my grandmother died, we bagged up her belongings. Her room became my room. I slept with the yet-to-be-trashed detritus of a life fully lived."

"And?"

"And they *moved,* Mr. Wong. The stuff and junk my grandmother left behind moved. I tore open the bags to look."

The Inheritor snapped its beak.

Bong-Cha didn't turn. "And my grandmother's things looked back at me with unearthly eyes. They spoke to me with voices unheard in decades. They told me of their long waits to inhabit the cast-offs of living beings."

"Long waits? People chuck out their junk all the time."

Her smile darkened. "Oh yes. And yet each one waits in its

disembodied spirit form for eons to find a host in a cast-off item. It shows you just how many of them are waiting for an entry into this world."

I pushed my hat back. "So how do I stop them, doll?"

"Ah there. You don't Mr. Wong." She reached out and caressed my cheek softer than any lover had. "You don't stop them at all."

"I take it you're in cahoots with the garbage gang?"

"You put it so vulgarly, Mr. Wong."

I pulled my hat down. "Usually."

"I am their milk-mother and life bringer. I engender them with bodies – bodies the world sees as junk. I give them strength and force and hardness. And they give me …" She trailed off into a dark smile. If she had a moustache, she would've twirled it.

"And they give you what?"

Darker smile. "They give me their fealty. They give me their obedience. They give me their undying devotion."

I pushed my hat back. "And what kind of orders do you give them to obey?" I asked, already knowing the answer.

"Ah there. You want an example? Oh yes." She turned her smile to the Inheritor, who smiled a beaky smile back. "My progeny – kill King Wong. Rip his sinews from his bones until no living being could ever recognize him as human." She smiled. "But bring me his hat."

三

22

The pile of black garbage bags heaved and undulated, unseen hands stretching the plastic to oil-slick green, then tearing it open. Then the cast-off collections of fat cat came at me with the full fury of those thrown away, forgotten and given supernatural life to come back and take revenge on humanity.

Razortoothed comic books bat-flapped at me, taking bites out of my jacket. Old records, taloned and bladed, buzzsawed past my all too unprotected head. Tiny silver spoons leapt from shredded trash bags and pounced on my shoulders, holding fast my ears with tiny silver arms, newly grown.

And, with my head immobilized, I got a great view of the cats.

What looked like twelve and a half thousand porcelain cats – their cutesy faces not enough to contain the monstrous teeth Bong-Cha's hopped garbage spirits had given them – marched in strict military column formation toward me.

I tried to step back. No dice. Tiny silver arms on more tiny silver spoons than I could count held my ankles.

I pulled my hat over my eyes. “Come on, Bong-Cha. It doesn’t have to be this way. What’d I ever do to you?”

She smiled. “You – and the rest of humankind – cast me off. When I told everyone of the beings I found in grandmother’s things, they sent me away. The tests I had to endure. The indignities of being locked up with the truly insane.”

“Rubbed off on you, did it?”

“No,” she snapped back. “I am clearly the sane one in an insane world.”

I pushed my hat back. “Right. No crazy person ever said that before.”

“Your kind cast me off. But I came back stronger.”

“What’s all this *your kind* business. You’re as human as I am, doll.”

She cast her head down and her eyes up at me. I didn’t like the look on her face.

“I was cast off, but I came back stronger. I came back better. I came back *more* than human.”

She seemed somehow taller. Larger than life-sized.

“I came back the first of a new breed – part human, part Otherkind. All powerful.”

She towered over me, her back hunched under the weight of the big blue turtle shell she just grew.

"And, as first of a new breed, I am the true Inheritor of this Earth. All will be but playthings for me and my progeny."

I struggled to get free again. No dice. I pointed to beaky shellback. "If you're the Inheritor, doll, who's this joker?"

Her smile got truly worrying. "This?" She gestured at the thing who called itself the Inheritor. "This creature is but a ruse to bring you to my mountaintop nest where my progeny will rip your limbs from your living body. It no longer has a purpose."

She reached out elongated fingers and wrapped beaky in her grip.

"My mistress – what have I done to displease you?"

"It can be disposed of," she smiled without answering.

In a motion, she lifted the giant beaked turtle into the air and cast it down the steep, jungled side of the Peak. It tumbled through underbrush and rock, sending bits of broken shell flying off into the trees.

She turned to me, her eyes wild and inhuman.

I pulled my hat down. "I take it I'm going for a tumble, too?"

"Oh no, Mr. Wong. I would never cast you off as you humans cast off so many of your precious belongings. I want to give you my *full* attention."

I pulled at my legs. Still no dice. "Oh, I don't want to bother you. I'll just take the same treatment as beaky, there."

"Silence!" She boomed, and it shook the mountain.

"Okay. Sure. No problem." I pushed my hat back. "Silence it is."

Her face darkened. "You're still not being silent."

"No, but I'm *telling* you I'm going to be silent. That counts, right?"

"Counts as silence? It does not."

"Okay. I'll be silent."

She smiled. "You won't be silent, Mr. Wong. You will scream to be wiped from the face of existence when my progeny tear at your living flesh." She stepped closer. "But still you will feel each nerve snap, each sinew wrench and rend, each muscle fibre slip and tear from your too solid body."

"So no easy tumble down the hill?"

"Not for you, Mr. Wong."

"Then at least tell me what I'm dealing with here. How did these things start to obey you? Why didn't they just rip you apart like you're going to have them do to me?"

She reared back. "What did I do?"

"Yeah. What made them your slaves?"

"Slaves, Mr. Wong? I assure you, my progeny are no one's slaves. They obey not out of fear or captivity. They obey out of love."

“Okay. So why do they love you so much?”

She stepped closer. “I showed them compassion, you fool. They had been cast off and forgotten by humankind. I showed them acceptance. They had been reviled by their owners. I showed them love. The *Dokkaebi* are no one’s slaves – they, the cast-offs of humanity, will be the masters of those who threw them aside.”

“Thanks, doll. That’s what I needed to know.” I pulled my hat down. “I call on you, Otherkind of the Borderlands, by your true name – *Dokkaebi.*”

A cacophony of screams shot through the air. I didn’t stick around to find out from who.

With my feet freed, I ran careening down steep Chatham Path, away from fat cat’s place and the rest of his now-murderous collection.

I heard Bong-Cha – the Inheritor – over my shoulder. “This is not the end, Mr. Wong. You think you can stop me by simply naming my progeny? You think you can stop me at all? We’ve already won. We are everywhere humans throw away what ceases to be useful. We are everywhere there is waste and overconsumption. We are humankind’s shadow – seldom noticed but everpresent. We have already inherited this world. We are the true masters now!”

“Yeah,” I heaved under heavy breath. “I’ve heard that before.”

The sheer act of saying anything broke the concentration I needed to move at speed down this grade of incline, and I lost my footing, mumbling over myself onto the broken asphalt.

I was up fast, but not fast enough. Behind me, a trash bag tumbled down the road, shooting out bat-comics and buzzsaw records as it went.

Then more. Bong-Cha stood on a ledge above the road and heaved fat cat's cast-off collections down at me.

Armies of Kewpie dolls, armadas of Matchbox cars and an air force of air mail stamps showered down on my head, defenceless but for the cracking straw of my hat.

They marched on me, and beneath the sound of their footfalls, wheels and flapping I heard a rumble.

I pulled my hat down over my eyes. "Let's see if this still has any power left in it, shall we? I call on you, Otherkind of the Borderlands, by your true name – *Dokkaebi.*"

A faded-faced Kewpie doll looked stunned, then laughed at me.

"A pitiful attempt, fool king," it said in a strangely butch basso. "Our numbers are so many that your meagre Foursquare naming magic won't work on us."

The rumbling rumbled louder.

I pushed my hat back. "Thank's for the intel ... um ... doll. But I only needed a small distraction."

It bared razorteeth from its cutie pie mouth. "Distraction?

For what?”

“For this.” I hopped onto the side of the passing haulage truck. “Change of plan, pal,” I shouted through the open window to the driver. “Best to leave these jokers where they lie.”

“We will end you, fool king. We will rip sinews from your –”

“Yeah, yeah. Rip sinews from my bones, pull my arms off and use them as puppets. I’ve heard it all before, chuckles.”

The haulage truck rumbled down Chatham Path and into the relative safety of traffic on Magazine Gap Road.

23

Darkness had fallen by the time I made it back to Nathan Road, which meant everywhere was bathed in the false dawn of neon signs advertising things folks don't need that they'll soon thrown away.

I shuddered. And I may have screamed at an old granny taking our her trash.

I slopped myself down at the bar of the Violet Eyes and poured myself a shot of Meyer's rum. I thought better of it and poured myself another.

"Tough case?" Jaz said from behind me.

I didn't turn. "The toughest."

"Tell me about it."

"You're just saying that so you can tell me about *your* day."

"Not *just*. But, yeah, that's part of it."

I pushed my hat back. "Tell away, Jaz."

I heard a smile cross her face. “Okay, so I totally decluttered all my stuff that I got traveling. I mean – I can’t believe I was hauling all that around.” She stretched her arms high above her head. “I feel so free. Like I can breathe easier.”

I downed my rum and spun around. “The stuff. Where is it?”

“What?”

“The stuff. What you got rid of. Where is it?”

“I put it in the back.” She crossed her arms. “Don’t worry – I’ll take care of it.”

“Not if it takes care of you first.” I ran to the door and recoiled. Hands and claws and teeth scraped at the porthole window.

Jaz was behind me. “What is it, King?”

I pulled my hat down. “By my best reckoning? The end of the world, doll.”

“That’s bad. And don’t call me *doll*.” She took me by my shoulders and turned me to her. “And how are you going to stop it?”

“I don’t think I am. Not this time.”

“Then who can? You know people, right?”

I pushed my hat back. “I don’t know anyone with this kind of firepower. This is Jade Emperor level stuff. Well, I guess technically I *do* know him, but.” I shook off the memory of the Jade Jerk. “Best I can tell, these things have been around since humanity first tossed away a spent fire stick. But they've never been organized. Not until Bong-Cha."

"Bong-Cha? Like, the decluttering guru?"

"Oh, yeah. You missed all that. Turns out Bong-Cha is half Otherkind. And all nasty." I pulled my hat down. "Like I said all along."

"Ugh."

"You said it, Jaz."

"So there's nothing? We just sit around and wait for the end of the world?"

I sidled back to the bar and poured another Meyers. "Until one of us gets a better idea. Yeah, that's the plan."

"No."

"What *no?*"

"No. I'm not going to do that. I'm going to do all I can to stop whatever bad guy is threatening to end my world this time." She looked me hard in the eyes. "And what I can do best is get you to act."

"Acting's great, Jaz. But I need something to act on. I've got nothing."

"No."

"Again with the *no*."

"Yeah – again with the *no*." She crossed her arms. "There's something. I know you. You've got an idea – even if you don't know you do yet."

"I told you – I've got nothing."

She put soft hands on my weary temples. "Don't push. Don't try. Just let your mind go blank. There must be something that whispers to you."

I cocked an eyebrow. "Do you really think this is going to work?"

"Shush. Just listen to your thoughts. See if something whispers to you."

I heard the clock tick and my stomach rumble. Then.

"Oh, Jaz."

She smiled. "You have something, don't you?"

"Yep. But I don't like it."

She pulled away from me. "Will it work?"

"I have no idea. Maybe." I pushed my hat back. "Yes. If I can pull it off. But the risk."

"Will it save the world?"

"Could. Or it could make this world completely unrecognizable."

"Is there another way?"

"Nope. These things are already anywhere there's human junk. So ... everywhere."

She crossed her arms. "Easy answer. The reward outweighs the risk. You know what you have to do."

"It's still a big risk."

"It's a big reward – saving the world and all."

"I don't know if I have the chops."

"Then who does?"

I pulled my hat over my eyes. "Not a living soul on this planet."

"Then it's you who has to do it. Easy answer."

"I'm not sure I'm up for taking the rap when I blow up all life."

"Are you up for taking the credit if you save all of humanity?"

Another slug of rum. "I'd prefer not to."

"If you're dodging the credit, dodge the blame, too."

I pushed my hat back. "I like you, Jaz. You keep me honest." I downed the last of my rum. "And I'm going to need some pretty darn pure and honest motives where we're going." I pulled my hat down. "Let's go."

24

The cut-rate lipstick and garish eyeshadow still glared against fluorescent lights like they always had, but I could see unease in how the staff moved. I found my favourite shop girl.

She saw me, too – and B-lined in the other direction.

I cut her off at a wall of knock-off perfumes with names like Lidl Suddenly and Sun Fragrant Water.

"She can't see you now," she said before I asked.

I pushed my hat back. "I know, doll. She's high-tailed it back to the great forest in the sky. I'm not looking for her."

She slit her eyes. "Then what?" Arms crossed. "Cosmetics? Yes, you could use a makeover."

"Another time, maybe." I pulled my hat down. "I need to get down there."

Arms tighter across her chest. "Not without her there."

"But she's not there."

"Then neither are you. *Joi gin.*"

I took a step closer, and she cowered. I pulled away and pushed my hat back on my head. "Look. Doll. Honey. Sweetie. It's urgent. I really don't have time for this."

Jaz put a hand on my shoulder. "King? Step away. You're not helping."

I pulled my hat down. "We don't have time for the softly-softly approach."

"We do. Because without it, we're not getting to where you need to be. Get it?"

"Hm."

Jaz turned to the shop girl. "What's your name?"

"May Lee."

"That's beautiful. I'm Jasmine. Jaz."

I stepped in. "We don't have time."

"How long has he been coming here?" Jaz said to May Lee, ignoring me. "Has he ever asked your name?"

"Not in seven years."

Jaz shot me a look. Then back to May Lee. "Ugh. That's atrocious."

I pushed my hat back. "Atrocious? That's a bit of an overstatement. I just got nibbled on by razor-toothed collectibles. *That's* an atrocity."

Jaz didn't turn. "So I get why you're not too keen on helping him. Totally understand. It's just that. Well." She turned away.

May Lee stepped toward her. “What? Is it that bad?”

“It is. It will be. Or *could* be, I guess.”

Worried deepened on May Lee’s face. “Is there anything I can do?”

“No. I can’t ask that of you.” Jaz looked to the ceiling. “Unless …”

“Unless what?”

Their eyes locked. “Unless you can get us down to the Underlibrary.” Jaz turned away. “No. I get it. I wouldn’t want him down there alone, either.”

“It’s my job not to let anyone down there when the mistress is out.”

“I understand.”

“I can’t even tell you that the lift only operates with something natural – something living and growing and vegetative. That’s its secret.”

Jaz smiled. “No, and I certainly wouldn’t ask you to tell us anything like that.”

May Lee blushed and turned.

I pulled my hat down as Jaz turned to me. “Not bad. I guess.”

“Not bad?”

“That’s what I said.” I scanned the pink storefront. “So all we need is some kind of plant? Like a flower or something?”

My eyes alighted on every variation of garish tropical

flower imaginable, all of them just printed on plastic and paper.

"That may be a bit of an issue in the concrete heart of Kowloon, Hong Kong."

I turned. Jaz was gone.

"Let me guess – you're going to sweet talk some plants to grow super fast for us?"

She popped up behind me with a sprig of what looked like a leaf with caterpillars growing off it.

"*Yiu!* That's nasty," I said and pulled back.

"But it's alive."

"Where did you find that? We're only a few blocks away from Tsim Sha Tsui pier in one of the most densely populated spots in the world."

Jaz shrugged. "Life still finds a way." She gestured out the pink storefront. "Look."

As my eyes accustomed to the dark from the glare of fluorescence, I saw weeds growing from the sidewalks, houseplants hanging from windows and tress lining Nathan Road.

I pushed my hat back. "Huh. I guess I built up Hong Kong so much in my head as a place of concrete and desperation, I missed what's actually here."

"Now are we going to do this?" Jaz said.

"Yeah." I took another eyeful of unexpected greenery and pulled my hat down. "Yeah, we are."

I led her to the lift. The smell was still there – deep forest cedar, sage and wet life – but there was an undertone of rot. The gross decay after an extinction event, where nature reclaims the flesh and matter we all only borrow. As the lift went down, it again expanded onto the forest, but this time the dark forest of nightmares or gnarled fairy tales. The leaves on the floor slushed under my feet, rotting into the corruption of nature.

The lift doors opened, but there was no lift left. Just the dark forest half-obscuring the ornate carved doors hung off their hinges, while unlit torches smoked in their sconces.

"King?" Jaz said. "This isn't how you described it."

"Not anymore, Jaz." I pushed through the hanging door, half expecting to find to find Cha Fa reclining on her *chaise*, cleavage on display to anyone who cared for an eyeful.

But there was nothing.

Deep purple rage welled up inside me. In a double handful of hours, I'd lost two of the people who made me who I am. Dr. Rodney – kind to me at a time when not a lot of folks could find reason to – and Cha Fa – she who led me through the cracks in the world to where all the things live that make life worth living.

But the whispers of millions of mystical books stored and indexed from the dawn of the universe calmed that rage, simmering it into hate. And a plan.

The whispers got louder.

"Jaz?" I pulled my hat down. "Do you hear that?"

"Hear what?"

"That's what I was afraid of."

Whispers.

I looked down and saw it – the dog-eared paperback with a faded image of a buxom dame on its cover.

"I guess it's time, doll," I said and opened the book.

25

Whispers caressed through my thoughts, reading them, but also forming them, making me think their will was my own. I pulled at my ears to rip the sound from them – no dice. These whispers were inside my mind itself.

Time and space folded backwards under me, and I was again in the halls of the Jade Palace, His holy Jade-ness flashing his all-light form in front of me. Jerk.

"You've returned to open the Whispers, Mr. Wong." He transmogrified into Dr. Rodney and pulled at his hair. "Did you learn nothing from your near miss with the *Xiezhi?*"

I pushed my hat back. "I'd hardly call it a near miss, Jade Jeans. I think I stuck my defense dead to rights."

"You're certainly entitled to your opinion. Even if it is the opinion of a human."

"Look, chuckles. I'm having a bit of a bad day. Aside from

our little *tête-a-tête* with your horny dog-thing, I've been nibbled on by comic books, attacked by flying records, lost a dear friend, had another run off to the woods and had my perceptions messed with by some big, blue, turtle-y decluttering dame. Any other day, I'd cut you down with a withering quip. Today? Today I think I'll just politely ask you to step aside and let me do my thing."

"No."

"*No?*"

"No. I cannot let you use the Whispers to remake this universe in your own image."

I pulled my hat down. "Believe me, pal – that's not what I'm doing."

"I can sense fear in you. Do you fear power, King Wong? Perhaps you'd be more content remaining a powerless mote of human dust?"

"That's not what's got me shaking, you Jade Jerk." I took a step toward him. "Let me whisper it to you."

I mentally collected the swirling Whispers in my head and sent them, murmuring, humming to the Jade Emperor.

His eyes went wide.

"No," he said.

"Again with he *no*. Where's all your enlightened positivity? You need more inspirational cat posters."

He pulled at his hair. "Do you realize the implications?"

"Yep."

"The cost? Do you know what that will do to Otherkind?"

"Yep. It'll wipe out the *Dokkaibei.* What else do I have to lose?"

His eyes darkened. "You know very well what you have to lose. Your very existence."

I pushed my hat back. "Yeah, well. It wasn't much of an existence to begin with. What's one King Wong more or less in the world?"

"When it comes to what you're planning, quite a lot."

"Meh." I pulled my hat down. "Now are you going to stand back and let the gentleman do his thing?"

"No."

I pushed my hat back. "Here we go."

"No. I will *help* you."

"You? Help me? I work alone, chuckles." I looked at him. "And why would you want to help me?"

"I have seen the coming of the end time. I never thought it would be this way. I thought I could hold it back." He cast his eyes down. "I know now there is no stopping it."

I pushed my hat back farther. "Well, them's the breaks, Jerry Jade-o-lot." I turned away. "Just hypothetically, how would even be able to help me?"

He smiled. "There is a word whispering in your head. A single word. Are you able to make it manifest – to say it with your pathetic human voice – in exactly the way it whispers to you?"

"Sure. Seems easy enough."

"Then by all means try."

"M – Wait. Let me try again. M-foo-gu-lah." I looked to him. "How was that?"

His smile deepened. "Not quite. Do you have some kind of hatred for unicorns?"

"Unicorns? No, why?"

"Because with your mispronunciation, you have wiped all unicorns from existence."

"That's hopped up. Unicorns don't exist."

He pulled at his hair. "Not anymore. And now they have never existed. The Whispers have unmade them throughout all time. All because of your clumsy human tongue."

"Fine. Maybe I need a *bit* of help pulling this caper off." I pulled my hat down. "But it sure doesn't need to be from you."

"No human would fare any better than you at making the Whispers manifest."

"Fair point."

"And no Otherkind would willingly be party to this foolhardy plan."

"Also fair."

"That leaves me." He pulled at his hair and smiled Dr. Rodney's smile.

I pulled my hat over my eyes. “And I couldn’t ask for a better sidekick to rewrite existence.”

“Shall we disperse with the sarcasm and get to the … matter at hand?”

“We shall, Green Jeans. We shall.”

“You already hear them. The words you need. But you hear others as well – static meant to stop you from your task.”

He was right. It was like trying to listen to every conversation on a packed MTR train in every language at the same time. “You sure know a lot about this.”

He pulled at his hair. “I have been in your position. I incanted the words that brought about the creation of the universe last time.”

My concentration on whispering words snapped. “Last time? How many times have there been?”

He smiled. “But back to the words, yes?”

I refocussed – trying to single out sounds in a language no human has ever spoken amid the cacophony.

His holy Jade-ness took a step closer. “The Whisper you’re looking for is shy, murmuring in the back, away from its brash, cackling compatriots.” He pulled at his hair. “Can you hear it?”

I could. “I can.”

“Focus on its sounds. Repeat them to me, but only to me. Do not let the universe hear.”

“What?”

“With your full intention, repeat the sounds only to me. Use intent not to let the universe overhear. I will correct your pronunciation, and you can then speak the proper incantation to creation.”

“Whatever you say, chuckles.”

I listened to the shy Whisper at the back, focussing on its near-unintelligible noises.

I repeated them, trying to focus only on the Jade Jerk. “Guh-nay, wa-showa, mi-necks-ee-too-din-us.”

The Jade Emperor closed his Dr. Rodney eyes and incanted. “*G’nei w’xoua minexitudunus.*”

And I repeated them back, full cheezy actor voice, hoping the universe would hear me. “*G’nei w’xoua minexitudunus*.”

Silence. The Whispers stopped.

I stood, probably with gaping mouth, looking at nothing and everything.

The Jade Emperor pulled at his hair. “It is done.”

“Done? That was it? The *Dokkaebi* are gone?”

He laughed. “Oh, you are so human. No. Everything is as it was. Now, as the universe’s new creator, you must create it.”

“Okie-dokie. Got any Silly Putty?”

“Not with your hands. With your thoughts. Will what want, find the thread that will make it so, and the Whispers will manifest it.”

I pushed my hat back. “Just like that?”

He pulled at his hair. “You make it sound easy.”

“It’s not?”

A smirk. “Start with something simple. Your heart’s desire, perhaps?”

Before I was conscious of what was going on, I was thinking of her. *Longing* for her. And the Whispers heard me.

26

You know that feeling you get when you read from an ancient mystical tome that recreates the universe exactly how you want it, and you bring back the long-lost love of your life? It felt exactly like that as I looked into Mei Hu's scared, darting eyes – now human, now fox, never settled. Whispers faded on the cool air of the Underlibrary.

"Mei Hu." I grabbed her shoulders. "It's me."

Wild eyes looked into mine. "No. It's not."

I pushed my hat back and took a long breath. "It is. This is real. You're back."

Her eyes darted. "It's not." Back to me. "It's not real. *You're* not real. I'm ... I shouldn't be here."

"That's the thing, sweetheart. No, you *shouldn't* be here. But you are. Because of me. I'm the one who shoved *should* where the sun don't shine."

She tried to hold my gaze, but her eyes darted like a wild animal. "Say that's not true. Please be lying to me, sweetie."

I pulled my hat down. "Lying? I'm not lying. I made this happen. I brought us back together."

"That's not possible."

I pulled my hat down further. "I don't care what's possible. I made it happen." I looked away. "Me."

Her eyes settled on mine and settled looking human. "No. Tell me you didn't, sweetie."

"Tell you I didn't what?"

"The Whispers. Please tell me you didn't use the Whispers. Please tell me Leng Cha Fa didn't give in to her soft spot for you and let her guard down. Please tell me it's not the Whispers. Anything but that."

Silence.

"Please, sweetie. Please tell me you didn't use the Whispers."

"I made this happen. I brought you back from ... wherever you were." I wanted to say *with whoever you were with,* but I swallowed the words.

"I was dead, sweetie."

"That's what everyone tried to tell me. I wouldn't believe them. Now I'm right."

She reached out to my cheek. "You're not listening. I was dead."

"No."

Fox flashed in her eyes. "Yes."

"How?"

She turned from me. I pulled her back.

"How, Mei Hu?"

"I told you my people saw a threat coming to them. It was bigger than we feared. The threat was to all Otherkind. A mass extinction event, but worse."

I pushed my hat back. "What's worse than mass extinction?"

She looked hard at me with fox eyes. "You, sweetie. You're worse than simply extinguishing the lights of all Otherkind. You're the one the ancients foretold of. You're the one who will make it so none of us ever existed."

"Not to contradict anyone's ancients or anything, but that's not going to happen. I'm going to make one tiny alteration to the way things are. Just enough to clear out the *Dokkaebi*."

Her eyes turned human. "And bring me back."

"Okay, *two* little alterations. Then everything goes back to being good. We go back to being together."

"No."

"What *no?*"

"No. It does't work that way. This is the Whispers, sweetie. Did you think it would be that simple? That you could just wish away what you didn't want and wish back what you did? You know Otherkind – is wishing ever that simple?"

I pulled my hat down. "I brought you back. It worked."

"Bringing me back is different from keeping me back."

"I'll do that, too."

She touched my cheek again. "Against my will?"

"Why, Mei Hu? I want to be with you." I squeezed the book in my hand. "And for once in my miserable little life, I have the power to make that happen."

"Power, sweetie? Would you take what you will by force and power?"

"If I have to."

"Even me?"

I didn't answer.

"Where's the ridiculous human I fell madly in love with after nine hundred years of seeing everything this universe can show me?"

"He's gone, sweetheart. He's been gone since you left."

"But you could bring him back, right? You have the power."

"Maybe I don't want to. Maybe I like who I've become since you ran off into the woods with fox boy. I've changed, you know. I've seen some of what this universe can show me, too. And most of it isn't pretty. Maybe I don't want to lose who I've become."

"Of course you don't." She looked away and looked back

with fox eyes. "So you can understand why I don't want to lose who I've become, either."

"You've become dead."

"Yes."

"And you want to stay dead?" I pulled away from her. "You'd rather die again than be back with me?" I snapped.

She stepped toward me. I pulled back.

"It's not like that, sweetie. You don't understand yet, do you? I'm dead *because* of you."

"What?"

"I'm dead because my people saw a threat to all Otherkind, and that threat was you. I couldn't live with that knowledge. I left my people. And –"

"And what? Killed yourself?"

She stepped toward me and I let her. "It doesn't work like that. You'll understand when you get to be nine hundred years old." Her eyes turned human. "So I suppose you'll never understand. My existence isn't about blood and beating heart. My existence – the existence of all Otherkind – is about will. As long as I will it, I go on. When I lose that will ..."

I pushed my hat back. "Mei Hu – don't. We can just be together. I remade the universe so we could be together."

"I can't be here, sweetie. You know that. Put things back the way they were."

"No."

"If you don't, I will. You can't keep me alive by force."

"Mei Hu."

"I know." Her eyes turned fox. "But it's time."

I opened the book. Whispers flowed from it, and I focused on Mei Hu again, but in the opposite direction. I focused on her leaving me, and her running to the forest. I focused on her gone. I focused on her dead. I focused on the lousy world she left me – a world of cockroaches, hopping corpses and garbage that springs to life when you're not looking.

The Whispers whispered my thoughts into words, those words into reality.

And, again, Mei Hu was gone from my arms as if she'd never been there.

Time and space folded back on themselves, and I was back in the Underlibrary with Jaz.

Jaz looked at me. "Did it work?"

I pulled my hat down. "Mixed results. But I'll tell you what – I'm mighty pissed off, and I'm itching to take it out on a certain decluttering diva demon."

27

Righteous rage is an interesting thing. Unlike other rages – like the feeling of flying off the handle – righteous rage is a calming force. It soothes you into knowing what you're about to do – no matter how violent – is for the betterment of all things.

Of course, righteous rage might be an out-and-out liar.

The Whispers whispered in my ears, asking me what I wanted without words, coaxing out my desires without questions.

I pulled my hat down further over my eyes. "Bring me the thing that calls itself Bong-Cha. Or the Inheritor. Or whatever. Bring her here and now."

Whispers of obeying raised me high on heady power. I clenched my fists.

Jaz put a heavy hand on my shoulder. "King? Are you alright?"

I pushed my hat back. "Just peachy, doll."

"You don't look good." She crossed her arms. "And don't call me *doll*."

"I'll call you whatever I damn well please. And I have the power to make you like it."

"King? What's going on?"

"I told you – all peachy."

"I doubt that. Because if you ever talk to me like that again, you'll get to know the business end of my knee quite intimately."

I laughed a hollow laugh. "You're going to threaten me?" I held up the Whispers. "I've got the power to change everything about your existence to suit my needs."

She uncrossed her arms and stepped toward me. "So do it."

"What?"

"Change me how you want me to be. If you're so unhappy with how I am, make me who you want me to be."

"Jaz." I pushed my hat back. "I'm not feeling so well."

"You've looked better."

"Maybe it's this place."

She put a hand on my shoulder. "Can you use your book-y power to bring us somewhere a little more familiar?"

"Chunking Mansions?"

"Always."

Without needing to say anything, the Whispers heard my

thoughts. Without any sensation of motion, we stood in an alley behind Chunking Mansions.

I smelled a waft of grease trap and garbage. "There's no place like home."

A shrill voice shrieked behind me. "Ah there. This place will be nothing like your home when my progeny rule this world."

I turned. "Bong-Cha. Inheritor. Whatever you're calling yourself today." I pulled my hat down. "That's not going to happen. Not while I'm here. See, I'm the world's only exoterric consultant. With two *R*s. I'm the one who makes sure big baddies like you don't start feeling yourselves, get all uppity and overstep the line." I traced a line in the damp asphalt of the alley with my toe. "And this is the line."

"Fool king, you are nothing. Less than nothing. You are *human*." She smiled. "Oh yes."

"Why does every two-bit, would-be, petty-tyrant Otherkind keep spitting that word at me like it's an insult?"

"Ah there. There is nothing lower than human." She stepped over my imaginary line. "Oh yes."

I pushed my hat back. "Now you've gone and made me mad."

She reared back, half hidden in her turtle shell, and laughed. "Ah there. Do you think the anger of a human frightens me? I have at my right hand countless armies of progeny your people have cast off and discarded. Your anger is nothing to my kind, fool king."

"Why do you keep calling me that?"

Her head jutted from her shell. "Because you are the fool king from the ancient prophecy of the *Dokkaebi*. A fool will rise to kingly heights, but for a day. Then this fool king will be stricken down."

"And you think that's me? The fool part I get. I've been called worse." I pulled my hat down. "Recently. But what about me makes you think I'm kingly?" I gestured to my rumpled linen suit, torn and filthy from pulled down Nathan Road by a hungry backpack. "Aside from the name, of course. Did you know *Wong* means *king*, too? Yeah, I bet you knew that. You seem like the type to know that. Is that why you called me the fool king? Must be." I scoffed. "Typical."

"Ah there. You're attempting to clutter my thoughts with stuff and nonsense."

"Me?" I pushed my hat back. "What could I possibly do to clutter your head? You're the decluttering diva." I stepped toward her and looked up into her now-twisted face. "But think about it – what does a king have?"

"A king has power. Oh yes. Power to bend the world to his will."

I gripped the book of Whispers. "And do I have power to bend the world to my will?"

"You are but human, fool king. Oh yes."

"There's that name again." I pulled my hat down. "But you didn't answer my question – do I have that kind of power?"

"Ah there. You have nothing."

"Well, that's not entirely true, doll. I've got a book."

She scoffed. "What can a book do against the cast-off army of clutter?"

"Quite a bit when it's this book."

I held up the dog-eared paperback, and she recoiled.

"Ah there. The fool king has stolen the Whispers."

"Not stolen. I … liberated it."

"Oh yes. And what will you do with the power of the gods, fool king?"

"Just this."

I closed my eyes, and the Whispers heard me. They danced around the edges of my mind, listening to my thoughts, my wishes. Then they shot out into the world, into time, tracing back the lines of *Dokkaebi*, finding the place they began, searching for the moment to write them out of existence.

Then I found it.

I opened my eyes. "No," I whispered.

Yes, the Whispers whispered back.

Bong-Cha smiled.

Jaz put a hand on my shoulder. "King? What is it?"

Bong-Cha shifted in her shell. "Ah there. Tell her, fool king.

Oh yes."

Jaz did a poor job of looking calm. "Tell me."

"They're the first, Jaz. They're what all Otherkind sprung from. Every god humanity has ever worshipped, every devil we've ever reviled, every household deity we've ever prayed to – all descended from the *Dokkaebi*."

She didn't speak. She knew what that meant.

I told her anyway. "So if I wipe all *Dokkaebi* from existence, I wipe every Otherkind away with them."

"That's bad."

"Worse than bad."

Bong-Cha snapped a smile at us. "Ah there. The fool was raised to kingship, but for a day. Now he is cast lowly again." She raised her eyes and hands to the towering buildings around us. "Oh yes. Now arise, my progeny, and take this world as your own."

From the dumpster behind us, from every apartment window and from the rows of souvenir stands rose the animated bodies of junk – cast off, forgotten or even just unsold – transformed into nightmare shapes of razor, barb and claw.

They swarmed the buildings of Hong Kong – and I'm sure everywhere else in the world – like ants on a dropped ice cream cone.

I clutched the Whispers hard in my hand.

28

With no sensation of movement or journey, I stood under the red sky in the primeval sludge of a planet giving birth to life. This planet. And from the bloody struggle of evolution, I saw the uncounted cast-off beings, life forms no longer viable for the cut and thrust of red-toothed existence. Gone, but not ended. Beings – entire *species* – extinct but retaining the basic animal will to live. Any life they can get.

"Otherkind," I said to no one but the sulphurous air. "All Otherkind are *Dokkaebi*. Every cast-off pattern of evolution takes on a mythical life. Dinosaurs become dragons. Ogres spring from extinct Neanderthals." I took an unsatisfying drag from my pencil. "All those disappeared forms of life continue on in our myths. They become Otherkind." I pulled my hat down. "To end *Dokkaebi*, I need to end Otherkind as a whole." I squinted into the red sky. "Now, I am become death.

Destroyer of worlds."

Well that's an oyster that sticks in the throat. First, I needed to say some goodbyes.

A journeyless voyage, and the red sky of life's dawn slipped to sleek steel and glass hallways. I pushed the door and stood amid the clutter of Dr. Rodney's office.

He pulled at his wild hair. "King? So good to see you. I'm glad you came." He leaned in and whispered conspiratorially.

"Demons, King," he said too loudly and pulled at his wild white hair. "Demons, I say."

I pushed my hat back. "Demons, you say?"

"I say demons. Chasing me. I know too much."

"You might be right there, pal." I pulled my hat down. "But not for much longer. I'm going to take care of them."

He snapped his wild eyes on me. "For me?"

"For you, Doc. For everyone." I looked out the window onto the bustle of Central. "Well, for every human, I guess."

"You're a good man, King."

I pushed my hat back. "There'll be some that disagree with that assessment, pal. Quite a few."

"Let them rot."

I looked back to him. "Not even that." I pulled my hat down. "But you'll be better. Feel better. Think better." I laid a heavy hand on his shoulder. "No more demons chasing you."

"No more demons, you say?"

"No more, I say."

I turned. I reached for the door, but turned back for one last look. "Keep it light, keep it bright, doc."

And I was gone. Another voyage without moving and I was in the basement of Chungking Mansions at the Violet Eyes, its beer-brand mirrors and spilled alcohol reflecting me back to myself in less-than-flattering ways.

"Jaz?"

She popped out from the back. "King? Is it done?"

"Not yet, doll."

"When?" She crossed her arms. "And don't call me *doll*."

"Soon." I pushed my hat back.

She uncrossed her arms. "No. You're going to find a way to stop these baddies without wiping from existence the only things that make life worth living, right? Without ending everything good and magical and awe-inspiring?"

"There are plenty of things more awe-inspiring than Otherkind."

"Name one."

"Oprah."

A pained smile crossed her lips. "Maybe." She crossed her arms. "But you're not going to do it, right? You're going to find a way without ... without *killing* them. Right?"

"All Otherkind are *Dokkaebi*. All of them evolved originally from existence's cast-offs. So, to stop the Inheritor and her brood, I need to make it so Otherkind never existed." I pulled my hat down. "You won't know when it happens."

"What are you talking about?"

"Look, it's hard to explain. It's not like I'm changing anything. Well … except I'm changing everything. But it's not like it'll go from being one way to being another way. When I change it, it'll have *always* been the new way. Back to the beginning of life."

"Once upon a time there was magic. Then something happened and there never was."

I took a drag on my pencil. "What?"

"Nothing. Something I read in a book."

"But you get it."

"Sure." She took a step toward me. "And what will we do? Without Otherkind, what use does the world have for an esoteric consultant?"

"It's exoterric. With two *R*s."

"Esoteric sounds better."

"Meh."

She crossed her arms. "You didn't answer my question. What will we do? It's going to be pretty bad PR to have the only protector of Otherkind become their destroyer."

I turned away, caught my haggard reflection in a Guinness mirror and turned back. "Jaz. There's not going to be a *we*."

Her eyebrows shot up. "Explain that, buster."

"We met because of Otherkind. When Otherkind cease to exist – become so that they never existed – there's no chance for us to meet."

"We'll find a way. We have to."

I pushed my hat back. "Goodbye, Jaz."

"No. No goodbyes. No farewells, no *au revoirs*. This isn't the end."

I took off my beaten-up straw hat and put it on her head. "Not for you."

And, again, I was gone.

Without blinking, I was above the whole spread of Hong Kong, the teeming city busying itself beneath me. I saw the *Dokkaebi* swarming, and I simultaneously saw them crawling over the whole of human enterprise across our fragile globe.

I spoke in a voice that was not mine and yet belonged to no one but me. I spoke the words of the Whispers.

"*G'nei w'xoua minexitudunus.*"

And I thought. I thought of the end of every Otherkind being. Every fairy trampled under tires. Every dragon hunted, slaughtered, roasted and eaten. Every monster burned in its cave, every hero exiled by their community, every wizard laid low by their own hubris. Every god shrivelled and forgotten by distracted worshipers.

And they died. Every mythical being that had ever existed died, burning and screaming into the uncaring void of the universe. And then, there were none. And there had always been none. In the time it took me to think the thought, myths went from muscular realities to children's bedtime stories.

But I saved a special end for the Inheritor.

29

While all of Otherkind burned and screamed, I kept a thought for sparing the Inheritor. She was the one who made this happen – who weaponized Otherkind into a force of pure destruction and hate. I willed myself to her, and I was there.

With a new hat.

She snapped her turtle beak at me. "Ah there. You may have sent away my progeny, but I remain." Snap of beak. "Oh yes. And within seconds, your precious humans will have cast off enough junk and tat for me to rebuild my army."

"Not today, doll."

Snap snap. "What?"

I pushed my hat back. "They're gone. They're not coming back. Heck, they never existed in the first place." I gestured to the teeming streets filled with people going about the business of the everyday, paying no mind to big blue turtle lady. "Call for them. See if they answer."

She looked around, then back at me. "You exterminated all of Otherkind?" A smile crossed her beak as only beaks can smile. "You are a better man than I thought. And yet you spare me. Ah there. I knew there was something between us, King Wong. Oh yes." Her beak smile deepened. "Shall we rule this paltry world as king and queen?"

"No."

"No? Ah there. Then why spare me?"

"I have something different planned for you." I pulled my hat down. You drove me to this. You made me end the only things in this tooth-and-claw world that make life worth living. That make life magical. Possibly the only things I've … loved. You don't deserve to just be wiped from existence. You need something special."

"Oh yes? And what is that?"

I pushed my hat back. "Maybe *special* is the wrong word. You deserve something … normal. You deserve a fate so unremarkable that no one would ever look twice at you." Hat down. "Or believe your wild claims of eyes and voices in your grandmother's junk."

"Ah there. No wild claims, Mr. Wong. You saw."

"It's different now. *Dokkaebi* never existed. No Otherkind ever existed."

She snapped her beak. "But I remember."

"And I'm going to make it so only you ever remember. So only you know of the things in your grandmother's cast-offs. So only you believe in them."

"Hardly an extraordinary punishment. Oh yes."

I took a step toward her. "You don't think so? You'll be the only human in existence to know of Otherkind. And you'll tell people."

"And?"

"And they won't believe you. Ever. They'll think it's the ramblings of a little girl who's lost touch with reality. They'll label you. Perform tests on you. Shower you with a false sympathy that's really just relief it's not *them* who are crazy." Another step. "And the whole time, only you'll know that you had the destiny to become the Inheritor. If only. If only Otherkind truly existed. You could have ruled everything."

"Ah there. That knowledge will keep me strong. A flaw in your plan."

"It might." I pushed my hat back. "For a while. But then it will eat at you. Bite out holes of doubt in your crumbling mind. Make you start to believe maybe the others are right – maybe there aren't really ancient spirits who inhabit what we throw out. Maybe *you're* the one who's crazy. And that doubt will grow. It'll become a hole so big it won't be a hole anymore. It'll just be life. It'll be truth." Hat down. "And you'll accept their medicines and their therapy. And, with a little luck and a lot of work, you'll become just like them. Another drone in a Foursquare world." Another step. "Except for one thing."

Snap of beak. "One thing? Do tell, Mr. Wong."

"You won't truly be like them. You'll be missing the one thing that makes you *you*."

"Oh yes?"

"Belief in yourself. You knew it all to be true, but you admitted it wasn't true just to please them. No one comes back from that."

"Ah there. A nice little fairy tale, Mr. Wong. But do you have malice pure enough to sentence me to a life of stripped humanity?"

I held out the Whispers, close enough for her to feel its hum.

She turned away. "That is useless in your paltry human hands."

"Yep." I stepped closer. "For a paltry human like me, it would take, say, a tutor as powerful as the Jade Emperor himself to teach me to harness all this raw, universe-bending juice."

"Oh yes. It would, indeed."

Another step. "Well, paint my undies and call me a Van Gogh, but damned if I didn't have old Jade Jeans show me the owner's manual on this thing."

"No."

"Yep."

"You can't. You can't send me back. We can work together. We can rule this world and those in it. We can be king and queen."

I pushed my hat back. "Not interested. What would I do with a world?"

With that, I let the Whispers caress my thoughts, let them find exactly the one of a scared little girl who had just seen eyes and heard voices from her late grandmother's cast-off belongings. And I let them make that a reality.

I breathed in the air of Kowloon. I bathed in the hum of life on its streets. Then I was ready.

Until the Jade Jerk popped up behind me with the face of Dr. Rodney.

"You have done a good thing, King Wong."

I turned and pulled my hat over my eyes. "Nope. Not even close. And why are you still here?"

"The Jade Palace is crumbling, being forgotten by the multitudes throughout the centuries who have worshipped it – and me. But my celestial body offers some small defense against the ravages of non-existence. For a time. I will be gone soon."

"Have a nice trip."

"King Wong – you have sacrificed what you hold dear so that humans may live and thrive. In the celestial ledger, you come out ahead."

"Had to kill nearly as many as I saved."

He pulled at his hair. "But only *nearly*."

"Cold comfort, Jade-y."

"But there is one more move you have ready to even up the score, is there not?"

"Just one."

"You plan to end yourself. To write yourself out of existence as if you'd never been."

I turned away. "That's the plan."

He came around so I was facing him again. "May I suggest a different option?"

"Nope. I ended the entirety of Otherkind. No world where I exist is going to be livable."

He pulled at his hair. "What if I had you exist in no world?"

I pushed my hat back.

"What if," he continued, "I could grant you an end worthy of a hero? One where you could have the blessing of immortality without the burden of the eternal consciousness that comes with it?"

Hat down. "I'm no hero."

"You are not one who is authorized to determine that. Only the future may judge our days and ways, and we cannot know what laws it will use." He pulled at his hair. "For your actions here, King Wong, I will grant you a continued existence within the world of words. Your stories shall live on in books – along with the stories of the Otherkind you so solemnly protected. You shall go on."

I pushed my hat back. "Me be a character in a book? It's hopped up, but fitting, I guess. I never belonged in the real world anyway. I'm too old-fashioned, and it's too Foursquare."

He pulled at his hair, then the Dr. Rodney image slipped into a being of a pure light. "And now, King Wong, go quietly and with all you are into *logos*."

The light intensified. I felt a rumbling somewhere deep inside my being, like after eating expired Seven Eleven dim sum. Then I –

30

In the fluorescent-lit false-streets of some eternal shopping mall in the New Territories, the business of life went on – or was halted, depending on your view of eternal shopping malls – as usual. No one noticed the sudden lack of magic and myth in the air because it wasn't sudden. That magic and myth – until minutes earlier a true and present force in this world, had now never existed. This way of life was brand new, and also had always been this way.

A kid – age and gender easily filled in by the vague generalities of this new, mythless world – flipped idly through a dog-eared paperback with a faded image of a buxom dame on its cover.

"Did you read that?" the kid's companion asked, age and gender also unimportant.

"Yeah. It was pretty good. It was like – what if all those old legends and stories were real, right? Like, monsters from myth and stuff."

"Cool."

"And then there was this guy – like an old-fashioned kind of guy who wore hats and stuff and wasn't respectful – anyway, this guy was like the only guy who could see these monsters."

"That power'd be *awesome*."

"But that's the thing – it wasn't cool for him. Because like everyone thought he was crazy. But he knew they were real."

"My grampa says myths and all those old stories used to be real."

"Oh yeah?"

"Yeah. But then something happened."

"And they're not real anymore?"

"I don't know. I never really get what he says after that. He kept saying that they were real, but then like something happened, and after that thing happened, they were never real."

"What?"

"I know. Weird, right?"

"Totally."

Noisy, shopping-mall silence hung over them.

The kid thumbed his book. "So – wait. Myth monsters used to be real, but then something happened and now they're not real."

"No. Myth monsters used to be real, then something happened and now they were *never* real."

"That doesn't make sense."

"That's what my grampa says. I told you I never got it."

"They were *never* real, but they used to be. Huh."

"I bet your old-fashioned guy in your book would get it."

The kid scoffed. "I doubt it. He's pretty thick. I had the mystery figured out *way* before he did."

"Cool."

"Yeah."

The noisy silence hung again.

"Want to go throw coins on the MTR tracks?"

"Cool."

And they were gone, past the police sign warning *Beware of Your Belongings*. They were gone, leaving behind them on the plastic bench of an eternal shopping mall a dog-eared paperback with a faded image of a buxom dame on its cover. Yet another cast-off belonging of life where we measure time through the *stuff* we get rid of.

If anyone going about the business of their life in that eternal shopping mall cared to notice, they may have seen that cast-off, dog-eared paperback twitch and jump on the plastic bench. Or maybe that kind of thing doesn't happen in this world. And never did. Not anymore.

Compendium of Mythical Beings & Assorted Knowledge

(adapted from the collected works of the Underlibrary)

Diyu – *Diyu* (literally "earth prison") is the place in the afterlife where punishments are meted out in preparation for reincarnation.

Dokkaebi – Originating in Korea, the *Dokkaebi* are disembodied spirits who take physical in human-manufactured items that have been cast off. At various times they have been to help – increasing harvests or catches – or hinder humans – causing fires or droughts. *Dokkaebi* are heralded by a tower of blue flame.

Fenghunag – The *Fenghuang*, or Chinese Phoenix, is a mythical bird that appears at times of high grace or virtues, such as weddings of virtuous people. Its tailfeathers may often punish those with selfish motives.

Jade Emperor – The *Jade Emperor* is the first Otherkind. His origins are unknown, but it's believed he is one of the Three Pure Ones, the three primordial emanations of the *Dao*.

Kasa-obake - A kind of *Yaoguai*, the *Kasa-obake* originates in Japan and gets its physical form by spiritually possessing cast-off umbrellas. The possessed umbrella grows a foot, eye and tongue, and is able to locomote by jumping.

Leng Cha Fa – (the entry on the fox spirit Leng Cha Fa has been destroyed, probably by her own hand)

Otherkind – Otherkind are the mythological beings that co-exist along with the dominant humans on Earth. They generally resemble gods and beasts from various mythologies. They may have been worshipped in ancient times and could be the source of these mythological creatures. Otherkind, depending on their place of origin, are classed as Desertkind, Mountainkind, Underkind, etc.

Xiezhi – The *Xiezhi* is a goat-like beast that rams the wrongful party when it sees a fight and bites the wrongful party when it hears an argument. It's power to discern right and wrong has been used for centuries by the Jade Emperor to try both humans and Otherkind alike.

More KING WONG Adventures

Kiss of the Cockroach Queen

When an expensive-looking dame from Hong Kong's swanky Mid-Levels offers King Wong a year's rent to find her missing shady, financial-wizard husband, he takes the case with only the help of a backpacker and whatever allies he can muster from the mists of Chinese myth.

Bones By Breakfast

When King Wong's assistant – and friend – is kidnapped as would-be bride for an ancient being from before the dawn of time, he drops it all to save her. Now, he's tracking down ancient, mystical elements with the help of a sassy woman of the night and whatever allies he can muster from the mists of Chinese myth.

ThePrairieSoul.com/press
Jacksontron.com

King Wong & the Tiki Terror

A Micronesian god is causing trouble on Hong Kong's wilderness island – but is he more dangerous than a mob of angry humans?

A short King Wong adventure

元朗
綿綿冰
糖水甜品專門店
翡翠

九龍生活攝影器材
盈興隆
參茸海味零沽批發
廳
End
終止
翡翠茶餐廳
盈興隆
參茸海味
零沽批發
海味

www.ingramcontent.com/pod-product-compliance
Lightning Source LLC
La Vergne TN
LVHW052029170826
845678LV00018B/2185